# PARASITE PLANET

# Borgo Press Books by JOHN RUSSELL FEARN

*1,000-Year Voyage: A Science Fiction Novel * Anjani the Mighty: A Lost Race Novel* (Anjani #2) * *Black Maria, M.A.: A Classic Crime Novel* (Black Maria #1) * *A Case for Brutus Lloyd * The Crimson Rambler: A Crime Novel * Death in Silhouette* (Black Maria #5) * *Don't Touch Me: A Crime Novel * Dynasty of the Small: Classic Science Fiction Stories * The Empty Coffins: A Mystery of Horror * The Fourth Door: A Mystery Novel * From Afar: A Science Fiction Mystery * Fugitive of Time: A Classic Science Fiction Novel * The G-Bomb: A Science Fiction Novel * The Genial Dinosaur* (Herbert the Dinosaur #2) * *The Gold of Akada: A Jungle Adventure Novel* (Anjani #1) * *Here and Now: A Science Fiction Novel * Into the Unknown: A Science Fiction Tale * Last Conflict: Classic Science Fiction Stories * Legacy from Sirius: A Classic Science Fiction Novel * The Man from Hell: Classic Science Fiction Stories * The Man Who Was Not: A Crime Novel * Manton's World: A Classic Science Fiction Novel * Moon Magic: A Novel of Romance* (as Elizabeth Rutland) * *The Murdered Schoolgirl: A Classic Crime Novel* (Black Maria #2) * *One Remained Seated: A Classic Crime Novel* (Black Maria #3) * *One Way Out: A Crime Novel* (with Philip Harbottle) * *Pattern of Murder: A Classic Crime Novel * Reflected Glory: A Dr. Castle Classic Crime Novel * Robbery Without Violence: Two Science Fiction Crime Stories * Rule of the Brains: Classic Science Fiction Stories * Shattering Glass: A Crime Novel * The Silvered Cage: A Scientific Murder Mystery * Slaves of Ijax: A Science Fiction Novel * Something from Mercury: Classic Science Fiction Stories * The Space Warp: A Science Fiction Novel * A Thing of the Past* (Herbert the Dinosaur #1) * *Thy Arm Alone: A Classic Crime Novel* (Black Maria #4) * *The Time Trap: A Science Fiction Novel * Vision Sinister: A Scientific Detective Thriller * Voice of the Conqueror: A Classic Science Fiction Novel * What Happened to Hammond? A Scientific Mystery * Within That Room!: A Classic Crime Novel * World Without Chance*

## THE GOLDEN AMAZON SAGA

1. *World Beneath Ice* * 2. *Lord of Atlantis* * 3. *Triangle of Power* * 4. *The Amethyst City* * 5. *Daughter of the Amazon* * 6. *Quorne Returns* * 7. *The Central Intelligence* * 8. *The Cosmic Crusaders* * 9. *Parasite Planet* * 10. *World Out of Step* * 11. *The Shadow People* * 12. *Kingpin Planet* * 13. *World in Reverse* * 14. *Dwellers in Darkness* * 15. *World in Duplicate* * 16. *Lords of Creation* * 17. *Duel with Colossus* * 18. *Standstill Planet* * 19. *Ghost World* * 20. *Earth Divided* * 21. *Chameleon Planet* (with Philip Harbottle)

# PARASITE PLANET

## THE GOLDEN AMAZON SAGA, BOOK NINE

## JOHN RUSSELL FEARN

Edited by Philip Harbottle

THE BORGO PRESS

MMXIII

# PARASITE PLANET

FIRST BORGO PRESS EDITION

Published by Wildside Press LLC

www.wildsidebooks.com

# DEDICATION

For Claire Jane King

# CONTENTS

# THE GOLDEN AMAZON

## by Philip Harbottle

In 1943 British writer John Russell Fearn decided to quit writing for the American pulp science fiction magazines, and to concentrate instead on books for the English market. Within a very few years he became established as a leading novelist in several genres, not only science fiction, but also mystery and detective fiction, and westerns.

His first new SF novel, *The Golden Amazon*, was published by World's Work in April 1944. In this story, a little girl of three years of age is made the subject of an idealistic scientist's illegal glandular experiments. The scientist's dream is to end world wars by creating a woman devoid of the usual lusts and frailties of mankind, who upon reaching maturity would institute a benign scientific rule. But the apparently successful experiment has a flaw: it instills into the girl a hatred for all men, and a ruthless cruelty. Her supernatural scientific gifts enable her to master atomic power, and practically leads her to destroy the world. She breaks the will and strength of men, and elevates women to positions of wealth and power. She also discovers human synthesis, and by this means she is able to escape retribution when she is eventually overthrown. She is seen to collapse and die, a victim of consuming ketabolism, echoing the memorable finale of Rider Haggard's *She*. In actuality, it was only her synthetic image, and this paved the way for the *Golden Amazon Returns*, and further sequels

Fearn sold reprint rights in the first novel to the prestigious Canadian magazine, the Toronto *Star Weekly*. The magazine carried a special Comics Supplement, the centre section of which was a 'complete novel', published in newspaper format. Aimed at a general readership, the novels were written by the top popular novelists of the day, including John Dickson Carr, Ellery Queen, and P. G. Wodehouse. They sold hundreds of thousands of copies, and the novels were syndicated to several American newspapers in the Maine and New York areas. The Amazon novels enjoyed extraordinary popularity (especially with Canadian housewives), and ran for the next sixteen years following the appearance of the first novel in the March 3, 1945 issue, ending with Fearn's sudden death in September 1960, aged only fifty-two. His final two Amazon novels appeared posthumously.

During Fearn's lifetime, only the first six novels were published in British hardcover editions from the World's Work in England, after appearing in the *Star Weekly*. This was because the publishers discontinued their entire fiction line in 1954. However, the Amazon novels continued to appear in the *Star Weekly*, eventually notching up twenty-four titles.

Fearn had resold paperback rights to the Canadian publisher Harlequin Books, but after publishing only the first three titles, they stopped publishing SF and other genre fiction to concentrate on their famous Romances line.

Meanwhile, as early as 1949, Fearn had realized that the Amazon series had the potential to run indefinitely. This presented him with a problem, however. The 'origin story' of the Golden Amazon was conceived and actually set during the Second World War. Subsequent novels were written during the war and the immediate postwar period, and projected their stories only a few decades into the future.

He very astutely realized that to keep ahead of reality, he needed to move the Amazon *further* into the future—first into the outer solar system, and thence to the stars. So with the seventh novel, he introduced a new main character, Abna of Atlantis—someone as equally intelligent, and even stronger than herself. These dynamics provided him with an *interstellar* canvas, thus ensuring that the series would remain ahead of reality.

Fearn's strategy was a great success, and the Amazon novels retained their popularity, ending only with his tragically early death in 1960. By then he had written a further twenty Amazon novels, and made prelimi-nary notes for his next (which would later be written by Fearn's biographer, Philip Harbottle).

Long after Fearn's death, his entire Amazon series

would eventually see print from the pioneering US small press Gryphon Books in limited paperback editions, and later by the Canadian Battered Silicon Dispatch Box small press in their hardcover Omnibus series.

This new Borgo Press paperback series will be the first trade edition of all twenty-one of these later novels by Fearn, beginning with the seventh novel in the original series. First published in 1949 as *Conquest of the Amazon*, I have edited it slightly as *World Beneath Ice* (The Golden Amazon Saga, Book One) so that it can be read and enjoyed by new readers who may be totally unfamiliar with what had gone before. Subsequent novels have also been slightly edited for modern readers.

The publishers hope that this new series may create many more "fans of the Amazon." Meanwhile, any reader interested in seeking out the earlier six Golden Amazon novels will find that they are readily available on the internet, and in numerous earlier paperback and hardcover editions.

\* \* \* \* \* \* \* \* \* \*

To date, readers can enjoy the following new Borgo Press editions:

**Book One: *World Beneath Ice***

In destroying the threat of an alien invasion, the Golden Amazon had inadvertently caused a decline in the sun's heat, encasing Earth in an ice sheet that threatens to eliminate humanity. The Amazon encounters Abna, a descendant of Atlantis, stronger and even more scientifically advanced than she, and the ruler of an Atlantean colony still surviving in a protected environment on Jupiter. She refuses his offer of marriage, but agrees to form an alliance in order to restore the sun and save the Earth. One thing that Abna has not told the Amazon is that all the females of his race have been wiped out by a bacilli infection....

## Book Two: *Lord of Atlantis*

A gigantic ridge of land rises from the Atlantic floor, causing massive tidal waves on either side of the ocean. Even stranger, both England and America are then assailed by an invasion of prehistoric monsters! A gigantic domed city rests on the newly risen plateau, whilst out in space an alien spacecraft orbits the Earth. Such are the mysteries and challenges facing the Golden Amazon, self-appointed governess of Earth, as she struggles to unravel the maze of mystery that was the deadly legacy of Atlantis!

## Book Three: *Triangle of Power*

The marriage of Violet Ray Brant—better known as The Golden Amazon—and Abna of Atlantis should have ushered in an era of peace and scientific prosperity to the people of Earth. But an unexpected turn of events finds Abna betrayed and marooned on a satellite of Jupiter, and the Amazon flung far beyond the Solar System. With Earth's two protectors removed, the planet is now at the mercy of another Atlantean, the master scientist Sefner Quorne....

## Book Four: *The Amethyst City*

The metaphysical union of the Amazon and Abna results in the mental creation of a fully mature daughter—Viona. Quorne, still struggling for domination, forces Viona into a marriage ceremony, and impregnates her. But with the intervention of Tarnec Brodix, a super-mind from an external universe, Quorne and Viona are separately flung into an ultra-dimensional limbo. Abna chooses to follow after his daughter, leaving the Amazon to brood over the disaster, alone in the Amethyst City of Saturn.

## Book Five: *Daughter of the Amazon*

A miscalculation by the super-mathematician Tarnec Brodix destroys his universe, and the fault spreads into the Earth universe in the form of a Dark Tide of Absolute Nothingness. Unable to save himself, Brodix transfers his knowledge into the one mind powerful enough to receive it: that if Sefian, the son who has been born to Viona and Quorne. Sefian rapidly evolves, and, no longer human, after saving the Earth universe, vanishes into the greater universe, to seek new challenges. Then the Amazon is confronted with a further puzzle—a large section of the planet Neptune is discovered to be an exact duplicate of the Earth!

## Book Six: *Quorne Returns*

The bacterial intelligences of Neptune plan to conquer Earth by replacing humans in key positions with alien duplicates. The Neptunians are themselves subjugated by the sinister Atlantean scientist, Sefner Quorne. Alerted to the threat, the Golden Amazon hits back by creating the ultimate doomsday weapon—only to precipitate a reprisal from the denizens of another universe....

## Book Seven: *The Central Intelligence*

The Golden Amazon's arch-enemy, Sefner Quorne, discovers that all mental gifts, such as memory and creativity, are something that is broadcast throughout the universe by a Central Intelligence—and then interpreted according to the quality of the individual brain of the recipient. At the surprising suggestion of his wife, Viona, the Amazon's daughter, Quorne travels with her to the very center of the universe, in order to wrest the secrets of mentality from the very source itself!

## Book Eight: *The Cosmic Crusaders*

The Golden Amazon renounces all ties with Earth when, together with her husband, Abna, and her daughter, Viona, she sets off on a journey to explore the cosmos. On the strange worlds of Alpha Centauri, she encounters Mizanu, the embodiment of evil—a planet-sized hypertrophied brain! Its baleful, crushing mental power threatens to reach out beyond the double-system of Alpha and Proxima Centauri to engulf the Earth and all the other inhabited planets of the galaxy—unless the Amazon can destroy it first!

# CHAPTER ONE
## INTO THE MILKY WAY

The *Ultra* was cruising at a leisurely speed of 40,000 miles an hour—a prodigious velocity by Earth standards, but a mere crawl to a machine which, under necessity, could exceed the speed of light itself by many, many times. Nor was this any familiar region in which the mighty space vessel moved. It was traveling in emptiness many light-years away from the Earthly solar system.

They had a self-imposed mission, these three who floated amid the stars, nor were three people better equipped to carry out that mission. The Golden Amazon; her giant husband Abna, metaphysical genius of Jupiter; and their daughter Viona made up a combination of scientific genius and superhuman strength possibly without parallel in the Universe. They called themselves "The Cosmic Crusaders," these three, their one aim to use their immense gifts to benefit the population of worlds that needed help or scientific education.

"Just the same," the Amazon commented, when the screens showed Axilon, their last point of adventure, as a mere pinprick of light, "we can't go on cruising like this with no main objective."

There was silence in the huge control room for a moment. The Amazon herself, the epitome of superb and ageless womanhood, was standing by the immense outlook window, every curve and line of her supernaturally perfect figure silhouetted against the stars.

Then Abna rose, seven feet of majestic strength, and crossed to her side.

"I seem to recall something about your saying the densest regions of the Milky Way might be a good area to head for next. Or have you abandoned the idea?"

"Far from it, Abna." The Amazon looked out to the misty, spawning swirl of the Milky Way with its incredible wilderness of myriads of stars, then her violet eyes turned to look at Abna.

"Far as I can see," the Amazon continued, "it is the best possible region where we might find other worlds. Out there, in this stupendous island-universe, amid all those spawning stars—there must be planetary systems. Worlds, maybe, that could benefit from our crusade to advance scientific amenities."

Abna nodded his blond head slowly, then gave a whimsical smile. The Amazon frowned. His whimsy was something she always found hard to tolerate, because she could never be sure but what he knew far more than she.

"I didn't think I said anything very amusing," she remarked briefly, and turned back into the control room, her very movements showing she was having difficulty in keeping her temper.

"Quite right, you didn't." Abna remained where he was, surveying her. "I was just thinking back to a time when you were a very different person, when your sole aim in life was to use your scientific skill to crush out the lesser factions and establish yourself as mistress of everything. Times have changed, Vi. Behold the beneficent empress," he finished dryly.

The Amazon swung. "You don't have to go back over the past, do you? Certainly my original aim was to dominate, until I found it paid better to make friends with people. I couldn't help myself in that. Part of my upbringing. It changed...."

"When I came along," Abna grinned, crossing over to her—and taking no notice of her petulant look, he grasped her shoulders and embraced her gently.

"Stop being primitive," the Amazon muttered, even though she made no attempt to pull away.

"Very pretty," observed a girl's voice, and Viona came from the corridor where she had just completed a rest period.

Abna and the Amazon disengaged themselves and looked at her—Viona of the copper-gold hair and sapphire blue eyes.

"Don't mind me," she smiled, lounging across. "I suppose it's natural for husband and wife to get affectionate sometimes. I wouldn't know. All I got for a husband was Sefner Quorne."

The mention of the dead Sefner Quorne, once Viona's husband, brought a grim silence for a moment;

then the Amazon moved into the gap.

"We were just saying, Viona, that the Milky Way might afford something interesting. Cruising around like this is pointless."

"I could have told you that long ago. All right, let's see what the possibilities are."

Viona led the way across to the multiple switch-board and snapped a series of buttons. Automatically, two things happened. The control room's atomic lights extinguished themselves, leaving only the soft glow of eternal starlight; and upon a big screen nearby there appeared a reflected image of the Milky Way picked up by the *Ultra*'s radio-telescope.

"Not much there," Viona sighed, pouting. "Or if there is, we can't see it."

"That's just the point," Abna commented. "We're so far away from the nearest stellar systems we can't sort them out properly. Only thing to do is narrow the distance. Set the computer to work, Viona. Let's see how far away we are from the nearest dense cluster of stars."

The girl restored the lights, then, switching on the computer, she fed it with the basic mathematics and waited while it electronically sorted them and finally produced an answer. The number of light years given in the totality display made the three glance at each other.

"Whew!" Viona whistled. "That's a stupendous distance in any language."

"We can cover it rapidly enough by exceeding the

speed of light by several times, traveling through hyper-space in the fourth dimension," Abna said calmly. "I'll set the course and fix the alarms to ring and waken us when we're reasonably near the cluster."

Abna computed the path through space, checking the figures by the infallible master computer, and then gradually swung the mighty vessel around until its nose was pointing directly towards the Milky Way. This done, he set the power plant in action and switched in the automatic control.

"Ready?" the Amazon enquired, and Abna nodded.

"Quite ready. We'd better get to the pressure-beds."

He, Viona, and the Amazon all stretched themselves flat on the pressure beds against the wall, beds in which the springs and cushioning were designed to expand and contract with the minimum of discomfort under extreme accelerative pressure. Then gradually the *Ultra* began to build up velocity, until it achieved that intolerable speed which brought down unconsciousness upon the three travelers. At the same time, entirely by automatic processes, the *Ultra* was plunged into hyperspace. In this region, the normal limitations on objects exceeding the speed of light no longer applied. Relative to the normal universe, the *Ultra*'s velocity steadily increased to the speed of light...and beyond it. Faster and faster....

# CHAPTER TWO
## THE PETRIFIED PLANET

As usual, the flawless design of the alarm system operated perfectly, and immediately several automatic controls came into operation. As the *Ultra* dropped back into normal space, the forward thrust of the power plant ceased and instead became retrogressive, slowing down the machine's incredible velocity through the deeps—and as the deceleration process continued so the Amazon, Abna and Viona gradually returned to consciousness as the strain was lifted from their hearts. They stirred, waited a few moments for final physical and mental adjustment, and then, without exchanging any words, they crossed to the great outlook window.

The view was incredibly changed from what it had been, A distant section of The First Galaxy—or Milky Way—was no longer an ocean of stardust and indeterminate points of light, but a vast, overwhelming mass of stellar systems.

The instruments showed that they had covered their huge spatial leap in a little over a week of Earth-time as measured in their ship itself, and that they were now within reach of the nearest stellar systems. But which system to choose in the midst of so many?

"The best thing to do," Abna commented, "is use a process of elimination. In other words, discard as useless the systems that do not contain features similar to our own. We want a system with a G-type dwarf sun, such as our own system has, and worlds with atmosphere similar to Earth's. Among this multitude we ought to find something."

The Amazon nodded silent assent and there began the task of setting the automatic analyzers to work. While the machines functioned the trio took the opportunity to refresh themselves after their enforced week-long sleep, and by the time this had been done the master-analyzer had gathered the computations of the "slaves" and produced an answer.

"Mmmm, sounds promising," Abna commented. "There is a system in the ninth quadrant from here, seven planets and a G-type dwarf sun. Each planet possessing oxy-hydro-nitrogen atmosphere, like our own earth."

"Ninth quadrant?" Viona repeated. "All right—let's head that way."

Abna and the Amazon knew she was experienced enough to handle the controls, so they moved to the window while she went to work. It seemed as though the ship remained motionless while the infinity of systems swung leftwards—then the course had been set and the radio-telescope was put in action. The perfect mechanics of the instruments made it that the required system was now exactly centered on the screen.

Abna and the Amazon crossed to Viona's side in the now darkened control room and surveyed the screen's image critically. The point that struck them immediately was that the system was somewhat unusual, in that there were six planets, all of similar size, so placed that they formed the six points of a hexagon. The instruments showed they were following a steady "follow-my-leader" orbit round the sun, each world exactly the same distance from it. The most surprising thing was that there was a seventh world, smaller than the others, comparatively close to the sun.

"That smaller world," Viona said, reading the instruments, "is 7,900 miles in diameter. I don't know whether it's coincidence or not, but Earth is exactly that diameter also. The other worlds vary between 9,200 and 9,800 miles diameter. The little world is about 70,000,000 miles from the sun, and the others are quite 100,000,000."

"Altogether a remarkable planetary system," the Amazon remarked, pondering. "The balance of it would be disturbed, you'd think, by that solitary inner world—yet everything seems in order."

"Whatever the peculiarities it looks like the right system for us to investigate," Abna decided.

The *Ultra* continued its onward journey, all the time reducing speed. Abna took charge of the actual control of the vessel while Viona and the Amazon made studies of the planetary system, and particularly its sun. Here again there was the hand of coincidence—or something, for in every particular the sun matched up with the dimensions and composition of Earth's own sun.

"Not that it ought really to be so surprising," the Amazon commented, studying the instruments. "There must be myriads of suns identical to our own G-type dwarf."

"Which, all things being equal, should mean planets having properties similar to those of our own system," Viona responded. "Soon find out, anyway."

It was, however, several hours later before the *Ultra* had come close enough to the unknown system for the radio-telescope to pick up details of the planets' surfaces. It appeared that the innermost world had the normal formations of continents, and oceans and clouds were few. All the other planets were shrouded in dense atmospheric blankets so no surface details were discernible.

"It looks to me," Abna said slowly, as the close-up image of the small inner world came back on to the screen, "as though that planet has considerable civilization, and of a fairly high order, too. Cities, observe? And those dots on the oceans must be seagoing craft. In fact, if it were not so ridiculous, I'd say that the formation of the continents looks curiously like those on Earth."

"Coincidence," the Amazon shrugged. "In any case, I'm not so interested in a world which reveals itself. I prefer the mystery of one cloaked in fog, like the rest of these outer planets. Since we're compelled to pass them first, we may as well stop at the one nearest to us."

So it was decided, and in due course Abna was lowering the great vessel out of the blazing sunlight into the dense fog of the nearest of the six outer worlds. The fog only thinned out after the instruments had shown a descent of two and a half miles—then there suddenly burst into view a gray view of landscape and the unmistakable signs of small towns and dwellings.

With scarcely a jolt, Abna finally brought the *Ultra* down in a clear stretch about half a mile from the nearest group of buildings.

"Everything's just right for investigation!" Viona exclaimed. "Gravity, atmosphere, humidity— We can go outside just as we are without trouble."

They paused only long enough to arm themselves, and then the airlock was opened. So similar was the exterior atmospheric pressure to that of Earth there was not even the sound of air escaping from the control room. Then, in that silent personal wonder which always possessed them when they set foot on an alien world, the three stepped out of the airlock and ankle deep into something that looked like the very finest gray ash.

Puzzled, they looked down at their covered feet—then at each other.

"What do you suppose this is?" Viona questioned. "Volcanic deposit of some kind?"

The Amazon unhooked a small scoop from her belt and gathered some of the substance into it. The tiny register on the scoop immediately analyzed the substance.

"Believe it or not," she said in wonder, "but this stuff is nothing else but dust! The undisturbed dust of time!"

"Dust?" Viona repeated. "But—but that's impossible! You don't get inches of dust lying like this in the open. Wind action keeps it moving...."

"There isn't any wind here," Abna said, in a queer voice. "*Look*! The clouds aren't moving!"

"I don't understand this at all," Abna confessed finally. "Let's keep moving. Maybe those trees over there can tell us something."

Their feet making no sound in the thick dust carpet, they headed to where four trees stood in an isolated clump. At close quarters they stood revealed as being of a species unknown on Earth, even though their general formation was normal enough. The extraordinary thing about them, however, was the bark, branches, and leaves. They were gray and petrified.

"Petrifaction of some sort," the Amazon decided at length, "though how it ever came about is a new one on me. Wonder if the same thing has happened to organic life?"

In general the town conformed to the standards of any town anywhere—where the civilization was not immensely advanced—and there were recognizable shops, dwellings, small parks—full of the same gray trees—and well-planned terraces. But nobody or anything was moving.

Finally Abna turned, his curiosity overwhelmed, and crossed to the door of one of the nearby stores. To his surprise the door was not locked, but he did notice it had a deadly coldness as he grasped the handle. Even more extraordinary, the door fell to bits and powder as he pushed it inwards.

Silent, fascinated by the mystery, Viona and the Amazon followed him through a short hallway and then into the store proper. And here indeed was the most astonishing sight of all.

Back on Earth the store would have been classed as an emporium, having a gigantic ground floor with countless sales tables and counters. Behind and before the counters were people, as motionless as the creations of waxwork. High up towards the ceiling was a curiously-fashioned clock, evidently stopped.

"By all that's weird!" Abna breathed at length, for once completely at a loss. "Look at them—stopped in mid-action. Look at that man there—"

"And the people are not so very different from us, either," Viona pointed out. "Similar in physique, even if their clothes are odd."

Abna began moving again and at length stopped before one of the women shoppers, who was apparently on the verge of accepting a package from the young woman behind the counter. Both women were fairly good-looking and both had thick black hair.

"Beyond me," Abna confessed at length. "Certainly doesn't look as though we can do much. Maybe we should move on and have a look at the other planets?"

"And leave a first-class cosmic mystery like this?" Viona objected. "Not likely!"

Suddenly Viona gave a cry of alarm. Immediately

Abna and the Amazon, at different parts of the store, glanced sharply toward her. She was standing at one of the large windows, gazing intently outside.

"Quick!" she urged, turning. 'Something queer's happening out here, and I think its dangerous! There's an invisible something making a trail heading straight this way."

In the distance they could see the immense bulk of the *Ultra*, and in the foreground to its left were the trees they had stopped to examine—but the strange thing was that something invisible was making a trail from the *Ultra* and hurling fountains of dust into the air in the process. A clear path was being cut in exactly the track they themselves had taken.

# CHAPTER THREE
## RESTORED TO LIFE

Within seconds the invisible something had reached the trees, then in further explosions of dust the trail blew itself to pieces and headed in a zigzag line down the main street and turned sharply into the very store where they now stood.

"Get ready," Abna said tautly, pulling his protonic gun from his belt. "Something invisible following our tracks."

They expected an attack from the invisible creature, but the three were for once mistaken. Fascinated, they watched the exploding trail, like fire following a line of dynamite powder, come straight to where they were standing. Then there was a violent explosion which flung them backwards from the window and sent them sprawling across the floor.

Before they had a chance to fathom what was happening, there followed a terrific thunderclap from outside and a cyclonic gust of wind. Immediately sound burst forth in the store—the chatter of voices in an unintelligible language, the movement of feet.

Slowly Abna got to his feet, staring around him as

he helped the Amazon and Viona up beside him. They were quite unharmed, but definitely bewildered. The store was full of movement and draughts. Outside, the frozen immobility of the clouds had passed away and they were moving before a strong wind, which was also carrying vast dust clouds along with it.

Then the shoppers caught sight of the unexpected trio and there came a breathless hush. Inevitably, a crowd began to collect around the three as they stood looking about them, guns still in their hands. Suddenly becoming conscious of this fact, the Amazon holstered her gun quickly.

In the distance the frozen 'clock' had moved onwards. Everything was incredibly, mysteriously in action again as though some unseen spring had been released.

*"Vadnia di kelnos excilit?"* asked one of the assembly in surprise, coming forward; and the trio studied him. It was possible he was the manager or proprietor, for the others—shoppers and what appeared to be salesmen and salesgirls—fell aside to let him pass.

"Your language is foreign to us," Abna responded, and the man frowned, obviously realizing he was hearing a tongue unknown on his world.

"Try reading his mind metaphysically," the Amazon said. Abna nodded and concentrated. It was plain the little man could feel the overwhelming mental power being trained upon him, but he stood up to it without panic. Then Abna ceased to concentrate and instead spoke, using the man's own language.

Back and forth the conversation went, the Amazon waiting in vague anticipation since she was not capable of reading thoughts to the same extent as Abna.

"It seems," Abna said at last, turning, "that there is a great deal more to this paralysis business than we realize, Vi. Our friend here is the store's owner—managing director, if you will. He's prepared to take us to his home where maybe we can knock some sense into things."

The Amazon made no comment, merely glancing over the open-mouthed, staring men and women who had congregated into a solid mass There were children, too, quite a few of them. Everything was surprisingly Earthly. So much so indeed that Viona felt stirred to a remark.

"I suppose we didn't go wrong somewhere in our journeying and land back on Earth in an unknown time?"

"You should know better than that," the Amazon retorted. "We didn't go wrong anywhere. Everything looks more or less on the Earth pattern because the basic conditions are similar. Same type of sun, same type of elements and atmosphere. That would automatically produce a similar form of life. No mystery about it. But let's get moving." she added, looking at Abna.

He nodded, spoke several strange words to the little man, and the trio followed him out the door.

# CHAPTER FOUR
## VIONA MEETS MEXONE

The home of the little man, whose name appeared to be Cesnon, was massive, well-kept, and on the edge of the town. And yet there was simplicity, and the three from Earth could not help but notice that there was no sign of television or scientific gadgets, even though there was an instrument in the lounge that was prob-ably a radio.

A meal of strange food, but tasty enough, was provided by well-trained and unobtrusive servants, then with the night drawing in, Cesnon led the way into the lounge with its big if rather archaic fuel fire, and here made introductions to his quiet and smiling wife and twelve-year-old daughter.

"I think," Abna said, glancing toward the Amazon as she reclined in a deep armchair, "that it would be better if I gave our friend here the gift of our own language—metaphysically, of course—then we can save time and energy. I'll just ask him if he has any objection."

The gibberish went forth for a moment or two between Abna and Cesnon, the wife and daughter listening in amazement and exchanging glances—then finally Cesnon spread his hands in a definite gesture of acceptance of Abna's proposition.

"He's agreeable," Abna said, as the Amazon and Viona glanced at him. "Won't take very long."

In a matter of five minutes it was over and the mental transference was complete. Abna relaxed again and smiled.

"You understand now?" he asked quietly.

"Yes...I understand." Cesnon hesitated for a moment. "You have the powers of a god, my friend, or else of a devil. With the gift of mental compulsion which you possess you could—"

"I could do much," Abna acknowledged. "That, however, is not the point at issue. My wife and daughter here—and I myself—have come from a far distant planet, as I explained to you earlier in your own language. What we wish to know is why we found your world petrified, and what brought about its return to normal."

Cesnon looked broodingly into the fire for a long time before answering; then he gave a little sigh.

"Frankly, friend Abna, I have not the least idea what caused the petrifaction—and as far as I have been able to gather since recovery nobody else seems to know the reason either."

"Not even your scientists?" the Amazon questioned, surprised, and Cesnon glanced towards her.

"Our science is not of a very high order, madam. Certainly none of our scientists were able to determine the nature of the creeping paralysis which finally over-took us."

"Then it did give a warning?" Viona put in. "It wasn't something that happened all of a sudden?"

"We knew for several—er—weeks that something strange was happening. Clocks were running slow; there was an unprecedented spell of cold weather, even though this is our summer, and almost everybody complained of a form of cramp. A sort of paralysis. But none of our scientists or medical faculty could account for it—then suddenly we experienced a blackout."

Abna frowned and then looked at the Amazon. She did not seem to notice him. There was abstracted distance in her violet eyes.

"I had rather hoped," Cesnon finished, "that my son might have been able to explain things, but apparently even he is at a loss."

"Your son?" Viona repeated.

"Yes, we have two children—Adza here, and Mexone. Mexone is twenty-three and very interested in the possibility of producing television. He is employed at the experimental scientific laboratories in the city."

"Possibility of television?" the Amazon repeated. "You mean you haven't established it yet?"

"No, there are many difficulties." Cesnon gave an apologetic smile. "I know we must seem a terribly dense-minded people to you, who are obviously from a civilization thousands of years ahead of us, but there it is!"

There was silence for a moment; then it was the

Amazon who spoke.

"We can possibly help you quite a lot to streamline your civilization, Cesnon, since that is our purpose. We are known as the Cosmic Crusaders, and our objective is to give a helping hand to those civilizations less developed than ours."

"A worthy and noble motive, madam," Cesnon smiled.

"But," the Amazon added, "before we bestow knowledge, we have to be sure it will be properly used."

"You have nothing to fear from us. We are a peaceful people."

"I'm prepared to believe that, but I am left wondering if you have neighbors who are also peaceful. I'm referring now to the paralysis that overtook you. By no stretch of scientific imagination can I believe it was a natural cosmic occurrence. It defies all normal laws. But it could be induced by scientific means of a high order...."

Cesnon was looking bewildered, and Abna and Viona exchanged a puzzled glance, then looked at the Amazon. As usual, her keen mind was ferreting for underlying scientific causes.

"Do you know anything of your neighbor worlds?" she asked. "You have telescopes?"

"Of a sort." Cesnon smiled ruefully. "I'm afraid they are not very powerful. The worlds near us reveal nothing in any case because they are cloud-blanketed."

"There is a further world near your sun where there is but little cloud interference. What of that one?"

"A moment," Abna put in. "Remember, Vi, that that world so close to the sun might not be visible telescopically because of the glare of the solar disk."

In the brief silence that followed there were sounds in the hall outside; then in a moment or two a young man entered. He hesitated in obvious surprise, only coming forward when Cesnon addressed him in his own language.

"My son, Mexone," Cesnon explained, and made the introductions as well as he could considering the language difficulty.

When he came to shaking hands with Viona, Mexone lingered for quite a time holding her hand. Nor did Viona withdraw it. She had already decided that Mexone was a good-looking young man—with the black hair which seemed to predominate on this world—keenly intelligent features, and thoughtful brown eyes. Then at last he relaxed his grip and smiled apologetically.

"I should think Mexone, as a scientist of this planet, ought to be able to help quite a lot," Viona said quickly. "But the difficulty is the language. Father, can you do anything?"

"Mentally transfer the language knowledge?" Abna asked. "Of course I can: it's up to Mexone. Ask him if he's agreeable, Cesnon."

The usual gibberish followed and it ended by Mexone nodding earnestly. It crossed the Amazon's mind for a moment that the young man was not so anxious to know the language for the sake of that alone as to be able to converse normally with Viona. Whatever his reasons, he submitted calmly enough to the impassive, hypnotic control of Abna as he mentally transferred all knowledge of the English language into the waiting mind.

# CHAPTER FIVE
## RANDOM ELEMENT

"Marvelous how you do that," Mexone reflected, when it was over. "Certainly nobody on this planet who's capable of it."

"I have done it," Abna replied, "because since you are a scientist you might be useful. We're endeavoring to discover the cause of the paralysis which overwhelmed all of you."

"So are a lot of other people," Mexone smiled. "The scientists in the city, for instance. Also, a lot is being said about you three wonderful people who've dropped in from outer space somewhere—where exactly?"

"A distance of countless light-years," Abna replied. "That is unimportant. Our aim is to help you, and it is just possible that you are being victimized without knowing it."

"Oh? By whom?"

"As yet I have no idea—but as my wife has pointed out, it is quite impossible for the paralysis on this planet to have been produced by natural causes. The only other possibility is that it was deliberately created."

"You are a scientist, Mexone," the Amazon said.

"Can you not form some theory as to how the paralysis was produced?"

"None at all. Nor can any of the other scientists. As I told you, our abilities do not yet rate very high, which is one reason why I can't believe anybody would wish to scientifically overpower us. We're beneath notice."

"That depends on what the unknowns have in mind. You have here a world that might be useful to somebody: your state of civilization doesn't enter into it." The Amazon pondered for a moment and then asked quietly, "Have you any knowledge of the process of entropy, of the meaning of thermodynamic equilibrium?"

"We do not understand, friends," Cesnon said, spreading his hands.

"What is this—er—thermo–something?"

"Thermodynamic equilibrium and entropy are virtually the same thing," the Amazon explained, "and they are states which apply to the whole universe and not to one particular world; therefore, the law is applicable to this planet as any other. Entropy means the running down of the universe, the state of increasing disorganization which must ultimately end in every trace of disorganization having been accomplished, when the death of the universe will take place."

Mexone and his father gazed in silence, completely lost. Abna gave a grin and glanced toward the Amazon.

"Your lecture-hall method doesn't fit the case," he told her. "Put it in simple language."

The Amazon sighed. "Very well, but it isn't going

to be easy. Imagine a deck of playing cards—or let us say a deck of cards with each one marked with a higher number. Card one is obviously 'one,' and so we go through the deck until we come to card number 100. Now to begin with, your cards are neatly stacked, with the 'one' on top and '100' at the bottom. That represents the point at which the universe began, when there was perfect order. But, from the moment of that beginning entropy—or disorganization—set in. The movement of energies, the interchange of forces, caused the perfect order to get more and more out of sequence. Our theoretical cards are no longer neat. We might have card 100 in the middle; card one at the bottom, and card 50 at the top. Clear, so far?"

"If you go carefully," Mexone replied, pondering.

"Finally, in any state of matter, there must come a time when every possible interchange of energy and so forth has been made. In other words, every possible exchange of cards—and that runs into tens of millions—has been accomplished and no more are possible. At that stage, the matter concerned is said to have reached thermodynamic equilibrium, which means that death has come. Total cessation of molecular movement, which is the basis of material life. The universe is more disordered today than it was yesterday, and this shuffling and reshuffling will continue throughout the untold centuries until eventually no more shuffling or reshuffling will be possible. When that stage is reached there will descend what is called 'heat death.' In plain language, that means that with the stoppage of molecular movement, heat and life will cease. It is only the activity of molecules and the energy interchange which keeps matter living."

"An interesting theory," Mexone admitted, "even if it does mean that the entire universe is hurrying onwards to doom, same as everything material. But how does it particularly apply to this planet of ours?"

"Expert scientists,' the Amazon replied, "could produce a localized thermodynamic equilibrium if they wished. I could do it myself in any laboratory. By forces which you do not understand in your present development, the molecules of any matter can be slowed to a standstill, bringing equilibrium and paralysis."

"Yes, I suppose that is possible, too," Mexone admitted, "but it is still only a theory, if I may say so. There's no proof that you are right."

"On the contrary." The Amazon leaned forward in her chair. "There is one more point regarding thermo-equilibrium which I must still explain. It is this: when that totally motionless state has been reached, it can be destroyed by the introduction of what is called a 'random element'."

"Random element?" Cesnon repeated vaguely.

"For the sake of our scientific illustration," the Amazon continued, "let us imagine the whole universe has reached the state of thermo-equilibrium and is dead, motionless. Now, from some source outside the known universe there comes either a radiation, a drift of matter, or a force of some kind. What happens? It would mean that disorganization would start up again, and life would gradually return to matter, because this new element would need to be shuffled and reshuffled through endless epochs until the balance was again restored....

"Our ship," she continued, "represented a random element introduced into a state of thermo-equilibrium. My husband, daughter, and I left the ship and walked through motionless dust to your store. The existing state of equilibrium was rapidly destroyed."

Silence. Then Abna spoke: "Since it is fundamentally impossible for one world to reach thermo-equilibrium while the rest of the universe remains normal, it seems to suggest that your world was deliberately put into that condition by scientific forces under intelligent control. The controllers of these scientific forces did not foresee the possibility of a random element in the shape of our advent. Unwittingly, we have undone all the work they built up."

"And," Viona put in, "there is one more point which supports the thermo-equilibrium theory. We found everything intensely cold, as far as actual matter was concerned. The air was warm, but that must have been caused by residual warmth remaining from the moment when the paralysis became complete—or even perhaps the air had still not quite succumbed to the general molecular slowdown."

"The latter theory is the more probable," Abna murmured.

It seemed quite an effort for Mexone to bring himself back to the realities of the moment after listening to such an airing of super-scientific knowledge. When he did finally find his voice, it was to ask a question.

"To all intents and purposes, everybody died. How did they come back to life and take up the thread just as they dropped it?"

The Amazon shook her head. "You did not die, my friend. None of you did. You suffered a form of suspended animation in which everything dropped to zero. But that has nothing to do with our immediate problem."

"Which seems to be to discover who produced such a disastrous state of affairs, and why?" Cesnon asked.

"Exactly."

"I still have no idea," Mexone sighed. "Unless, as you have suggested, one of our neighbor worlds might be responsible. To make sure it would be necessary for you, in your marvelous machine, to visit each one of them. As you have said, each one of them might, however, be in the condition that ours was until you came."

"My interest," the Amazon replied, "still centers on a smaller independent world near to your sun, which apparently you know nothing of."

Mexone looked surprised. "Is there one?"

"Definitely, and with a reasonable-looking civilization. There might even be science there of a high order. As to why your world and maybe the neighboring worlds have been subjected to such treatment, we don't know—but we can try to find out."

"Immediately?" Viona asked, and for some reason it

sounded as though there was a sharp edge of disappointment in her voice.

"Well, of course!" The Amazon looked at her in surprise. "I see nothing to be gained by delaying."

"Somehow," Cesnon remarked. "I cannot feel that it is right that you should have to endanger yourselves on our behalf—yet on the other hand, our science is of such a poor order that we are powerless to help ourselves. Naturally, it goes without saying that we're extremely grateful to you."

"Our governing body ought to know what is intended," Mexone put in. "So far everything has been confined to us, and we're only ordinary citizens when all comes to be said."

The Amazon shook her head briefly and got to her feet. "That, to my mind, would cause a lot of delay, together with endless explanations. There just isn't the time. I think you'd better do all the explaining yourselves."

"It will not be at all easy." Mexone was looking troubled.

"In some ways," Viona said, thinking, "I have the feeling that we're neglecting our job, mother."

"Meaning?" The Amazon gave her a sharp look.

"Primarily, our job is to help backward worlds to advance their civilization so it can have all the necessary amenities. For that very reason we call ourselves the Cosmic Crusaders. Here we have a planet definitely in need of an uplift, yet the first thing we do is dash away from it on the off-chance of tackling a planet about which we know precisely nothing. And on top of that, poor Mexone is left with the unenviable task of trying to explain thermodynamic equilibrium to the governing body. To say nothing of attempting to explain why we came here and what our object is."

The Amazon and Abna looked at each other. This was the first time in all their experience they had ever found Viona disinclined to leap into a new adventure.

"Of course," Viona added, rising, "there might be a way round it. I could stay here and impart such scientific knowledge as I possess, and you and father could go ahead to this mystery world. You don't really need me as well. You're quite capable of looking after yourselves."

"That is possible," Abna admitted dryly; then he, too, got to his feet, caught at Viona's arm, and drew her away to a quiet corner of the room.

"I'm afraid you're not doing it very well, Viona." Abna said, smiling. "I could read your mind and find out the truth, but I never invade the sanctity of thought unless I'm compelled. It wouldn't be because of Mexone that you prefer to stay behind, would it?"

"Of course not!" Viona's sapphire-blue eyes had a hint of resentment in them, but under her father's steady look the light died out of them. "That is.... Well, he's rather nice."

"Very. Quite a good-looking young man, but his intelligence rating is infinitely below yours, my dear—"

"All the better. You like being top dog. Well, so do I. Here's a young man I really like, and he hasn't enough knowledge to dictate anything. Not like Sefner Quorne, for instance."

"I see." Abna gave his slow, tolerant smile. "You haven't had much fun in your associations with the opposite sex so far, have you?"

"I can teach these people a good deal," Viona added.

"And Mexone too, maybe," Abna murmured; then he led the way back to the group and raised his voice. "I've just been talking things over with Viona, my friends, and I think it as well that she stays with you."

# CHAPTER SIX
## SCIENTIFIC ADVANCEMENT

"All this business is quite a wonderful experience for me." Mexone said to Viona, as they walked side by side. "That a girl so beautiful, and so scientific, should suddenly descend into the bosom of my family is something incredible. I half wonder if I'm not still paralyzed and dreaming it all. If I am, I don't ever want to wake up."

Viona smiled a little and glanced at him. "It's all real enough, Mexone—at least as real as anything material can ever be. I've been brought up on mental truths, remember, and because of that I make matter my slave, not my master."

"Oh...I see." The young man's hesitancy was obvious. "Well, anyway, thanks for offering to help improve our civilization. I will naturally do all I can to help. Where do you propose to begin?"

"The first thing you will need to do is convince your governing body—or else I will—that they need factories devoted entirely to the manufacture of machine-tools and instruments. Once we have those, the building of scientific equipment will follow. In time you will be able to have television, atomic power, all the benefits of electronics, and ultimately space travel. I know all the secrets, and once I'm satisfied yours is a civilization capable of using its benefits wisely, I'll hand those secrets on. After, of course, my parents have agreed. My first allegiance is to them."

"Yes—naturally." Mexone looked up into the night sky and toward the colossal backdrop of the Milky Way. "I must admit surprise that you so casually parted from your parents. You might never see them again!"

Viona laughed. "I shall. I know the powers they have, and I defy anybody in the universe to defeat them. I'll see them again all right."

Presently a thought struck her and she glanced at Mexone as he trudged beside her.

"How about aircraft?" Viona asked. "Have you any? Up to now I haven't noticed anything."

"Air flight is only just commencing to be experimented with. I'm sorry to have to keep apologizing for the backward state of our civilization, but— Come to think of it, though, it isn't backward at all!" Mexone's tone changed abruptly. "We've never lost a day in trying to progress. It is you who happen to belong to a civilization so far ahead of us. In the normal way we would no doubt reach your level eventually—but if you can give us the extra boost, all the better."

"I'll do that all right, with you as go-between and interpreter. How about your biological and medical sciences? Are they reasonably good?"

"Fair. We have many incurable diseases among us,

many of which could be overcome if we only had a way to see inside a body and discover what ails it."

Viona almost stopped walking in amazement. "You actually mean you haven't discovered the x-ray yet? Or its equivalent?"

"What does that do?" Mexone inquired innocently.

"Sees through solids. It's the very basis of much of our surgery back home; though in our advanced era medical surgery is becoming one of the defunct arts. Practically all disease is treated and healed by mental work, which at root is where the trouble starts. You're not up to that yet, so one of the first things you must be informed about are x-rays, and after that, aircraft which can move faster than sound itself—or super-sonic, as we call them."

"Faster than sound?" Mexone repeated incredu-lously. "Is that possible?"

"Every bit as possible as a space machine moving faster than light. You have much to learn, Mexone. You are entering on a new world of discovery, and your civilization will benefit from it immensely. In fact," Viona finished slowly, "it becomes essential that your people should learn the scientific arts as soon as possible. Only by that means can you defend yourself against enemies. And it would seem from the recent paralysis onslaught which overtook you that you have very real foes indeed."

"And if your mother and father dispose of those enemies?"

"There will be others," Viona sighed. "One is never

certain of peace as long as evil minds exist."

# CHAPTER SEVEN
## MYSTERIOUS DUPLICATION

To a machine capable of such prodigious speed as the *Ultra*, the journey to the inner world of the queer hexagonal-shaped system was not a long one. Indeed, in a matter of hours—even including their orbital surveys of the other planets—the leap over the gulf had almost been completed, and to the Amazon and Abna, watching the approaching world intently, there was unfolded yet another mystery in this extraordinary odyssey.

"There's no doubt about it any more, Vi," Abna said at last, as they surveyed the screen of the radio-telescope. "That world is an exact duplicate of Earth itself! Or almost, anyhow. The topography is dissimilar in places, but ninety percent of the layout conforms exactly to Earthly geography. But for the slight differences here and there, I'd swear anywhere that it is Earth itself. I never saw anything like it!"

"Four worlds with a reasonable civilization—five if we include the one we've visited," Abna summed up. "And one world back in the age of monsters and entirely undeveloped. Apparently the world we picked was the only one subjected to thermo-equilibrium, and somehow we've got to discover why."

The Amazon looked toward the inner world. "We don't know for certain, Abna, that that inner world caused the trouble. We're just playing a hunch."

"Soon find out." He switched off the telescope. "I think that world would be well suited to produce some devilment: it's so right off the track of the other planets and probably invisible to them.... Anyway, we'll be landing in about fifteen minutes."

And as the minutes passed and the inner world came nearer, there was no longer any gainsaying the fact that the main city of the "British Isles" of this world was exactly like London itself.

For quite a time the Amazon remained at the window, studying the patterned puzzle below while Abna remained at the switchboard; then, she turned suddenly and crossed to a computer terminal. From it she presently produced an aerial photograph and with it in her hand returned to the window and again studied the view, comparing it with the print in her hand.

"By all that's unbelievable!" she exclaimed finally, more startled than Abna had ever seen her. "Abna, come here a moment and convince me I'm not going crazy."

Abna switched in the automatic control and then did as bidden. In a few moments he had discovered the reason for the Amazon's profound perplexity. For the scene below was an exact replica of the photograph of London in her hand!

"Every building, every street, exactly as it was at the time I set about thinking of taking over London, and then the world," the Amazon said tensely. "I was sure I recognized it. Yet this photo was taken by me just about the time I had grown to womanhood and decided to use my scientific powers to subjugate the world. That's ages ago now—yet here is the same layout. For heaven's sake, what's the answer?"

"Beyond me," Abna said at length. "There's no denying the exactness between original and photograph, but at that time I didn't even know you or your planet, so I'm lost."

"Have we somehow returned to Earth in a past time, or—" The Amazon shook her head impatiently. "No, that can't be it. There is the backdrop of the Milky Way. We're incredibly far from Earth itself, and yet...."

"No use working yourself to pieces over it," Abna shrugged. "We'll find out the truth quickly enough when we land."

Abna said no more. He returned to the switchboard, cut out the automatics, and then began the process of gently lowering the huge machine. As he did so, it became evident that people below had seen the vessel descending, for there was a stirring in the streets and a general exodus from buildings. The Amazon stared blankly as upon the front of the immense airport building she could now distinguish the words—Trans-World Airlines. Yes, that very building had existed in the twenty-first century.

"English language!" the Amazon whispered, half

to herself. "That completes the picture, and makes the mystery blacker than ever."

Abna was too busy with the controls to pay much attention. He maneuvered the ship down gradually over the building tops and at last descended on a wide, clear stretch of the airfield. In an instant an army of mechanics and ground staff—all of them entirely human-looking—came racing into view.

"All very homely looking," Abna murmured, switching off the power plant. "But this isn't Earth itself, Vi—disabuse your mind on that. For one thing, the sun's much closer and bigger. Want me to open up?"

"Naturally." The Amazon took her gun from her belt.

Abna depressed a switch and the airlock began to open slowly.

"Apologies, Miss Brant," one of the approaching mechanics said. "We were not expecting you to return in a much larger machine than the one in which you departed."

The Amazon gazed fixedly, trying to sort out the meaning of the statement, even though it had been spoken in perfect English.

"In which I went away?" she repeated. "But I—"

"Quiet," Abna murmured, nudging her. "Accept what they say for the moment and lie your way out. This is intriguing."

The Amazon cleared her throat and the ground staff waited respectfully, even though they did seem inwardly mystified.

"I—er—have returned in this particular machine for various reasons," she replied. "With me I have brought a friend by the name of Abna."

"Your machine," the chief mechanic said. "Shall we try and put it—"

"Leave it here until further orders." The Amazon hesitated, right out of her depth. "I may need to depart again quickly. You can dismiss for the moment—except you," and she looked at the chief mechanic.

The rest of the men nodded and went off again to their various duties. The chief mechanic waited as the Amazon and Abna came to his side in the intensely hot sunlight.

"I have something to confess," the Amazon said slowly. "I have suffered an accident which has somehow affected my memory. Tell me.... When did I leave here and where was I supposed to be going?"

"You left here about a month ago, Miss Brant, but you did not say where you were bound for."

"Thank you," the Amazon muttered, frowning.

"Possibly," the mechanic finished, "you might gain better information from either Mr. Wilson or Miss Grayson. Will there be anything more?"

The Amazon shook her head but did not speak. In stunned amazement she watched the chief mechanic turn away and hurry after his colleagues.

"Now where are we?" Abna asked, surveying the airport with vague interest.

"Still up to our necks in mystery," the Amazon replied. "Not only is that mechanic—and presumably everybody else—sure that I set off a month ago from here, for an unknown destination, but now he refers to Mr. Wilson—"

"You mean it could be Chris Wilson, chief executive of the Dodd Space Line back on Earth?"

"I can't imagine any other Mr. Wilson. Listen, Abna. Early in my career, I did leave this airport, or its replica, for my scientific headquarters underground, before I launched the attack that was intended to destroy London. At that time I was using the first *Ultra*, the prototype of this monster I now possess. That seems to tie up with the mechanic saying he hadn't expected me to return in a much larger machine. On top of that, he refers to Irene Grayson."

"I noticed his reference to Miss Grayson. What of it?"

The Amazon's eyes were bewildered. "Irene Grayson was my mother, and in those days she was very much alive. I don't think I—I could stand meeting her again in the flesh. It's all too uncanny."

"Or else *duplicated*," Abna answered with his usual quiet assessment of scientific possibility. "Get one thing clear, Vi, we are definitely not on our own Earth. The sun alone is proof, so are certain differences in this world's topography—but I will grant you that we seem to have fallen amongst people who have the names and probably the appearance of people who were on Earth just about the time of your first climb to power. How it comes about we'll perhaps learn in time. I suggest we go and see this Mr. Wilson and see if he's anything like

Chris Wilson we know back on Earth."

The Amazon said no more. With Abna beside her, she crossed the broad spaces of the airport, noticing as she went that the various aircraft being serviced were definitely ancient models with none of the improvements she had later brought into being.... The interior of the airport executive building was also just as it had been far in the past, and to enter it was like some dream of exceptional clarity. So into the office of Chris Wilson himself, after a discreet knock on the door.

Once within the office, Abna closing the door behind her, the Amazon gazed fixedly at the solitary man within. He was dressed impeccably in a lounge suit and he was certainly Chris Wilson. Not the ageing, white-haired man who now ruled the far-flung destinies of the Dodd Space Line back on Earth, but an alert, spruce young man in the early thirties.

"Hello, Miss Brant." His voice was not at all cordial as he got to his feet. "You've returned, then...." The eyes of Chris Wilson II strayed to Abna's gigantic figure.

"Obviously I've returned," the Amazon retorted. "This gentleman is Abna, a scientific colleague of mine."

Wilson II nodded briefly and then waited. The Amazon struggled with confusing memories of past events and then tried the same excuse she had already used.

"My memory is a trifle faulty, Mr. Wilson, due to an accident I suffered recently. What plans had I made with you before I departed a month ago?"

# CHAPTER EIGHT
## AMAZON II

Wilson II smiled cynically. "I have never been aware that you entrusted your confidences with anybody, Miss Brant. I can only quote rumor—that you intend to implement your regime by the destruction of London if everybody does not do exactly as you order."

"I see." The quietness in the Amazon's voice and her general air of bewilderment was plainly puzzling Wilson II more than somewhat, but for all that he made no effort to be compromising.

"If there is anything else—?" he asked, hesitating.

"I'd like to see Miss Grayson," the Amazon said, and seated herself, Abna taking up position at her side.

Wilson II apparently had no objections to Irene Grayson being summoned, for he pressed a switch on his desk and spoke into an intercom. At length the office door opened and a tall, stately woman of middle-age entered. She hesitated, looking at Wilson II, then towards the Amazon and Abna.

"Miss Grayson?" the Amazon asked, struggling now with the stupefying realization that she was looking at her mother, whose death she had witnessed more than fifty years before!

"Why do you ask?" Irene Grayson inquired. "You know perfectly well who I am."

"Not altogether," the Amazon corrected. "I am having trouble with my memory due to an accident. I just wished to ask you if I made any special plans with you before I left in the *Ultra* a month ago."

"You made no plans with me, Miss Brant, and even if you had done so I would not have supported them in any form."

The Amazon got to her feet again and went across to where Irene Grayson was standing.

"You are my mother, are you not?" the Amazon asked slowly, and at that Irene Grayson gave a distinct start.

"How can you possibly know that?"

"Never mind how I know it; just answer the question. I know you'll answer truthfully because my mother was an honest and courageous woman."

"Was? Why do you use the past tense...? Yes, if the truth must be told, I am your mother, mother of the child who was subjected to gland surgery twenty or more years ago, and because of that became the dangerous superwoman who we know today as the Golden Amazon."

The Amazon laughed lightly. "Everything you are telling me happened more than fifty years ago, Miss Grayson. And none of it happened on this world, but back on Earth where the original Golden Amazon was born."

"But there is only one Golden Amazon!" Irene Grayson exclaimed.

"I think there are two—not only of myself, but of everybody who was on Earth at that particular time. I have not the least idea as yet how this complex riddle comes about, but we might get at it if we can contact the Golden Amazon of this world."

Irene Grayson exchanged a look with Chris Wilson II. He shook his head slowly and dubiously.

The Amazon shrugged. "I know what you're thinking—that I am mad, that the accident I referred to has unhinged my mind. I can assure you I never had an accident, and even if I had have done so my mental power is sufficient to heal myself instantly. I repeat, there are two Amazons. This world is duplicate of my own planet. Send out a radio call stating a second Golden Amazon is in London and see what happens!"

"It's incredible," Wilson II muttered, "but I'll do it just the same. I can sense there is something about this situation which isn't normal."

He snapped on the intercom once more. "Radio headquarters? Send out a world broadcast as follows— 'Second Golden Amazon in London. First Amazon's presence requested immediately.' Yes, that's it."

He switched off again and then sat in brooding thought. Meanwhile Irene Grayson was studying the Amazon with an intense gaze.

"I am something of a scientist," she said presently. "And for that reason—"

"I know you're a scientist," the Amazon interrupted.

"My mother was also a scientist, so it seems logical, since you exactly duplicate her as she was alive, that you will be a scientist too."

"I was going to say," Irene Grayson said deliberately, "that maybe this is an example of cosmic twinship. I've heard of it and wondered if it might be possible."

"Something like that perhaps," the Amazon admitted. "I have formed no theory at all as yet."

"This gentleman with you—Abna," Chris Wilson II put in. "I can assure you we have no duplicate of him on this planet. If we had he would be known by his very size and majesty."

"Thanks," Abna grinned. "Point of fact is, I was not on Earth at the time, so presumably I can't be duplicated. It seems that only those on Earth at that time have their replicas here. By this time Earth is some fifty years ahead, so to us it looks like a retrograde step in time."

"It isn't that," the Amazon said slowly. "Consider something, Abna. To get here in this region of space, we traveled many times faster than light. Light is the ultimate physical speed—and once you get ahead of it, time automatically goes backwards."

Abna nodded, but he did not offer any further theories. Even he was still somewhat overcome by the immeasurable mystery of the situation. And so, for a time, the conversation drifted into commonplaces, during which it became clear that the heavens to these people were utterly unlike the heavens seen from Earth. Proof yet again that this was not Earth, but some crazy duplicate thereof.

* * * * * * *

It was almost an hour later when the Amazon broke off her conversation and pointed through the window. There, heading down toward the airport, was a long gray ovoid.

"My first *Ultra*!" the Amazon exclaimed, but there was no astonishment in her voice this time. She seemed to have become reconciled to this profound mystery of duplication, exact in every detail and the prototype of the present vessel.

Irene Grayson and Wilson II got up and crossed to the window. For them too there no longer seemed any doubt of the fact that there must be two Golden Amazons, and the possibility was proved to the hilt when a few minutes later there entered the office a tall, blonde girl in black tights. Yes, this was a second Golden Amazon without doubt.

"What," Amazon II asked, in a cold, authoritative voice, "is the meaning of this masquerade?"

"It is no masquerade," the Amazon assured her. "You are me, as I was fifty years ago. At that time I was a cold, heartless creature intent on nothing but my own glory—just as you are now!"

"That is an insult!" Amazon II retorted. "Who are you? Where have you come from?"

"Earth—many light years away from here." The Amazon moved forward slowly. "Make no mistake, I am flesh and blood, and I have no intention of trying to imitate you. On the contrary, it would appear you are imitating me, perhaps without realizing it."

A slow change of expression came over Amazon II's beautiful face. The haughty anger died out of it and instead she began to look puzzled.

"Plainly," the Amazon said, "you are a scientist of no mean ability: you must be since you are possessed of as much knowledge as I was at the beginning of my career. Don't you think it would be as well if we retired into conference and sorted out this problem?"

"Very well." Amazon II gave a shrug and glanced towards Abna. "I assume he is to be included?"

"Certainly. He is my husband and, in some things, cleverer than I."

Amazon II smiled cynically. "That I do not believe. No man living can be cleverer than the Golden Amazon. But come, we can discuss best at my headquarters."

And, just as the Amazon had expected, the head-quarters proved to be a counterpart of those she had once had,

"This mystery of identicalness is, I think, only another phase of scientific development," the Amazon said, after thinking for a moment or two. "To search for the answer in physical causes would be useless. So that leaves us only the mental realm."

"Very well," Amazon II shrugged. "What's the explanation? I am prepared to listen while you explain. If I don't agree with you, I'll put forward a theory of my own."

"One thing I have discovered in my travels," the

Amazon said. "It is that there is no limit to the power of thought. There obviously cannot be, because it has not the limitations of matter and is eternal. A radio set, for instance, receives the same broadcasting station as another set if both sets are identically tuned. Agreed?"

"Elementary," Amazon II said, in some contempt.

"Suppose, then, that your brain and mine are absolutely identical in convolutions, synapses, ganglia, and so forth. Suppose your brain is, so to speak, a carbon copy of mine?"

"Or maybe your brain is a carbon copy of mine."

"Unlikely." The Amazon shook her head. "In years I am much older than you are, therefore I must be the original and you the duplicate. My theory is this: given identicalness of brain structure, it is possible my thoughts are yours as well."

Amazon II rose. "You intrigue me. Suppose we settle the issue of brain structure right now with the x-ray equipment? Then we can discuss further. Come—the laboratory's this way."

"I know," the Amazon said dryly, getting to her feet, and in a moment or two she, Amazon II, and Abna were within the long, low room that produced on the Amazon a strange 'I-have-been-here-before' feeling.

# CHAPTER NINE
## MENTAL PARASITES

The matter of taking the x-ray photographs was handled by Abna. Both women were dealt with and then the results were carefully studied and measured.

At the end of an hour there was no doubt whatever.

"Just as I thought," the Amazon said. "You and I have absolutely identical brains, one in sympathy with the other—at least as far as the reception of thought is concerned. The difference in your brain is that the areas commonly considered to be responsible for imagination, initiative, and so forth are absent."

"Which means they must be actually redundant," Amazon II decided. "I have imagination and initiative in plenty. That goes without saying, since I am the virtual ruler of this planet."

"I suggest that, but for me, you would not be," the Amazon said deliberately; and as the woman stared at her in amazement the Amazon added, "I'll even go further and suggest that not only you but everybody on this planet would be a mindless idiot were it not for the people of Earth."

"I assume you don't mean to be insulting?" Amazon

II asked coldly.

"I am stating what I think is a fact. Put more simply, for a reason you cannot help, you and your race are mental parasites. Physical parasites abound, the case of one organism unable to live without the life of the other—but in this case the order is in the mental realm. You think because I think, but if you had not my thoughts, you would be an imbecile. You would go on living because you are a distinct organism apart from me, but your mind is made up of my thoughts—as they used to be fifty years ago."

Amazon II was silent, pondering deeply. The Amazon herself reflected for a moment, then:

"Yes, the position begins to take shape. On this world there is a race of people who possess brains identical in general formation to those possessed by Earth people, with the one difference that the imaginative areas are missing. If there were not brains of similar formation in the Universe—namely those on Earth—these people here would be what we call hopeless imbeciles."

"I think you are absolutely correct," Abna said, "but it still leaves a lot unexplained. Why, for instance, does not this double of yours pick up your thoughts now while you're on the spot?"

The Amazon considered for a moment, then looked at her twin.

"Have you in your files any detailed analysis of the composition of this planet of yours?"

"Certainly I have." The cold, haughty manner had returned. "Here it is."

From a filing cabinet a complete dossier was produced, and the Amazon and Abna both spent the next half-hour studying it. Amazon II watched them idly but did not pass any comment. The expression on her face, however, was fully indicative of the annoyance she felt at having her supreme authority challenged in this fashion.

"Well, more pieces begin to fit into the puzzle," the Amazon announced at length. "This world, though composed of elements similar to those of Earth, does not emanate any magnetic energy worth mentioning. That is caused by your sun being so near, which absorbs what slight energy there is as fast as it is generated. By energy I mean the energy produced by the spin of your planet...."

"And how does that relate to your theory?" Amazon II asked.

"It relates in this way: we have discovered—my husband and I—in our spatial explorations that Earth emanates a decided amount of energy, which has the effect of capturing and amplifying both radio and thought-waves transmitted from Earth. Without that Earth-energy, the strength of most ordinary radio and thought-waves would be dissipated almost immediately. As it is, there is no reason why thought and radio waves should not pass far across the universe with undiminished intensity. Have you ever received radio messages in your own language? Or rather, borrowed language?"

"No," Amazon II replied. "Radio waves are difficult

to receive on this world because of the static interference from the sun. I imagine the same thing must happen to thought-waves."

"Not at all," the Amazon replied. "Thought-waves are of exceptional sensitivity and extremely short, for which very reason solar force would not interfere with them."

Amazon II considered, piecing together the pattern of the theory, then:

"What it amounts to, then, is that you believe Earth thought-waves are received at this vast distance for two reasons: one, because of the similarity of our brain structure; and two, because Earth transmits an energy which causes the thought waves to retain their original strength no matter how far they travel?"

"That's it," the Amazon conceded. "Thought waves flow outwards for evermore, encompassing the farthest reaches of space."

"That I can understand, but why should I receive thoughts from you which are in a time past? Some fifty years or so?"

"The time lapse is not really a problem at all," Abna put in. "The thought waves, having been captured and transformed by the Earth's magnetic energy, move at the speed of light—186,000 miles a second—which is the generally accepted law relating to velocities. My wife and I have proved that thought waves of themselves can exceed that speed, and are practically instantaneous. That was when we contacted a being called Tarnec Brodix, who was actually outside our own Universe. But that was only achieved by *concentrated* pure thought, which doesn't enter into our present calculations. The point is: ordinary thought waves that had been captured, transformed, and then relayed by Earth's magnetic field would, by all normal laws, radiate into space at the speed of light."

"And so?" Amazon II questioned.

"My wife and I came from Earth at many, many times the speed of light. Thereby, since we exceeded the speed of light for long periods at a time, we must finally have reached a point where we actually overtook all light and thought and radio waves sent from Earth. The farther we traveled at a speed in excess of that of light, the farther behind would fall the radiations from Earth, until by the time we got here we are only receiving the radiations of a past time—from fifty years ago, in fact. The other fifty years have still to catch up. We are that much ahead."

"Yes, that would seem logical," Amazon II confessed. "It also seems logical that bodies would conform in shape to the minds ruling them, which accounts for duplication."

"And, of course," the Amazon herself added, "since you use borrowed minds, you also build everything in exactly the same way that we did in the past. Even your general planetary topography looks like Earth's when seen from above. A lot of that must be purely coincidental, yet some of it has been caused by the very engineering acts which we performed fifty years ago, and earlier."

"All of which means that I shall automatically live your life as you have done?" Amazon II questioned; but after a long spell of thought the Amazon herself shook her head.

"Not necessarily. You will inevitably be receiving the thoughts I gave off fifty years ago, but you will not necessarily interpret them in the same way as I did. Only the people are duplicates: the conditions governing the circumstances around them might be very different. This is a separate system, after all."

"Reverting back to something else," Abna put in, "It becomes clear why our present thoughts have no effect. Since this world emits no energy amplification worth mentioning, our thoughts are dissipated. The effect is only possible to anybody living on Earth, where the amplification can take place."

"That's it exactly," the Amazon agreed. "Also, it would appear that—as far as we know as yet—this is the only world where mental parasitism is possible because of the brain structure of the people upon it."

Abna was about to say that their experiences on the nearby world where they had left Viona confirmed this fact, but a look from the Amazon silenced him.

"My only aim," Amazon II said slowly, clenching her fist, "is to rule this planet of mine, and later the rest of the worlds in this system. I'll do it, too, before I've finished."

"I had the same ambitions in the past," the Amazon said quietly. "You are simply repeating again the resolutions I made at that time."

"And naturally you succeeded?"

"No, I failed. I realized that super-scientific power is not the answer if one desires co-operation."

"I don't desire co-operation, only absolute control, and, though you have succeeded in convincing me that I am only a living creature afflicted with mental parasitism, I'll achieve my object no matter what."

"It would appear," the Amazon said slowly, "that you have already started to do that. We noticed one world afflicted with complete thermodynamic equilibrium. I assume that is your doing?"

# CHAPTER TEN
## UNEASY TRUCE

Amazon II hesitated for a long moment, apparently caught out for an answer. Then she asked a question herself: "I assume you have explored the six outer planets before coming here?"

"Only through the x-ray telescope. We particularly noticed the one that had been brought to a standstill, its people included. Only you, having the same scientific genius as myself, could have devised such a plan."

"Yes, you are correct." Amazon II moved across to one of the massive switchboards against the laboratory's further wall. "The answer lies in a powerhouse not far from here, controlled by these switches here. Voldas is the name of the world you are referring to."

The Amazon smiled whimsically. "Fifty years ago I once thought of such an idea, but did not put it into practice. You have the same notion, but have acted on it. That is why I said that your existence would not be a slavish copy of mine. Circumstances cause a change, of course. And your reason for so subjecting Voldas?"

"I have already told you. I intend master this entire system."

"How like an echo of my own voice," the Amazon sighed; then she looked up sharply as she found her double directly confronting her, her violet eyes hard with inquiry.

"Though my knowledge may be your own, Amazon One, tell me this: what do you intend to do on this world? Challenge my power, attempt to destroy me, or what?"

"At the moment," the Amazon responded, "I have no fixed idea of what I intend to do. We believe scientific power is not intended just for one, or two, or a few people, but for every living, thinking being. Call it the new gospel, if you like—or a cosmic version of 'help your neighbor,' but the fundamental idea remains unchanged."

"Which means you are here to destroy me because my science represents danger?" Amazon II laughed shortly. "I think you have more sense than try that, either of you. I know you are scientists on a par with myself—probably far ahead of me—but what I lack in knowledge I have in resources. Your limit is that giant spaceship with its mighty scientific weapons—oh, yes, I looked over it, believe me—but I have buried workshops all over this planet, and thousands willing to leap to my command at a second's notice. If you wish to pit power against power, I have no fear of the outcome."

The Amazon turned away thoughtfully, far more disturbed than she showed. Here was an astonishing situation: she was faced with a superwoman, just as scientific as herself, and one ruthlessly determined to have her own way. Abna, between the two super-women, made a brief effort to try and read the inner-most mind of Amazon II. In doing so he gave himself a surprise, for the woman's mind was impenetrable. It was not a real mind at all, but a reflection of thoughts from another mind, and therefore was immune to any probing whatsoever. Abna was grimly conscious of the fact that he was robbed for once of a mighty weapon—the ability to know the thoughts of a possible foe.

A light glowed on the nearby instrument panel and a voice spoke:

"The presence of the Golden Amazon is requested immediately in the main observatory."

Amazon II turned, frowned, then glanced at Abna and the original Amazon.

"I would ask you to pardon me a moment. We will resume our discussion afterwards. Wait here for me, please."

She left the laboratory and the door closed. Abna glanced about him, wondering if any microphones were installed, and also whether the interruption had been deliberately devised so the second Amazon could depart and then overhear conversation.

"Keep your voice down," Abna murmured. "Maybe a trick."

"Could be, but I believe it was genuine. And since the observatory wants her, it could be that the restora-tion of Voldas has been discovered. We can look out for trouble if that should be the case."

"Trouble?" Abna repeated, grinning. "From her?

You're losing your grip, Vi."

"On the contrary, I'm facing reality. When she said she has infinite resources by comparison with us, she's right—and knowing my own skill, I'm alarmed as to what she might do."

"Whatever happens, we're more than a match for her together," Abna whispered, but the Amazon did not appear too convinced.

"What has she in mind?" she murmured. "Have you tried to discover?"

"I've tried—futilely. I can't read a mind that only reflects thoughts without originating them. We're cornered on that angle. And incidentally, why did you stop me mentioning too much about Voldas? She's bound to find out sooner or later that it has gone back to normal."

"Maybe, but we don't need to take the blame for it, do we? And remember, we've left Viona there. We don't want to endanger her if we can help it."

Abna nodded slowly.

Meanwhile, Amazon II had reached the observatory. She looked questioningly towards her observatory director as he turned to face her.

"I thought you should know that our latest observations of Voldas, taken last night, reveal this."

The observatory director motioned to his assistants and the place was plunged into darkness. Then a projector started up and Amazon II watched in silence as there was depicted on the screen a view of a thriving world, the images from its surface being clearly revealed by use of x-ray penetration through the cloudbanks.

"Apparently." the observatory director said, as the film finished and the lights came up again, "something has gone wrong with your thermo-equilibrium system, Amazon."

"There can only be one answer," Amazon II said slowly, her eyes hard. "As you will be aware, two strangers have landed on this world, one of them looking exactly like me."

"Yes, I am aware of it. But how does it happen—?"

"It means they lied to me. They did not say they had actually visited Voldas, but now it seems plain that they must have done so, and by so doing they automatically provided a random element in the otherwise perfect balance and have undone everything I built up. They'll regret that!"

Controlling her anger with immense difficulty Amazon II swept out of the observatory and returned to where Abna and the Amazon were waiting for her.

"My apologies for having to leave you," she said. "A rather urgent matter came up. I believe, when I left, that we discussed our relative positions."

"Correct," the Amazon assented. "You were saying that what you lack in knowledge you can make up in resources."

Amazon II smiled a little. "I was angry then; I confess it. Now I have had a moment or two to think, I realize that there is little to be gained by having enmity between us."

"You mean," Abna remarked, "it is like the irresistible force meeting the immovable object?"

"You can put it that way...." Amazon II walked across to the nearest switchboard and set several controls and a master-switch. At that moment, in a distant underground powerhouse, there began the process which, by waves of energy, would again start the gradual slowing down of Voldas into a state of thermo-dynamic equilibrium.

"All I can do," Amazon II said, returning to where the two were standing, "is to endeavor to behave as a good hostess should—and I think you are both wise enough not to try conclusions with the resources I possess. As your hostess I am willing to take you on a tour of our system and show you what the various worlds contain. Once that is done, I shall expect you to go—for good."

"Why the conducted tour?" Abna asked, puzzled—and not a little chagrined that he could not read the woman's mind.

"Why not? You are scientists, interested in what other worlds contain. I have no desire to withhold information of that kind. I think you'll find this hexagonal-shaped system quite interesting. I do, though, ask a small return," Amazon II added. "I would like to make this tour in your own machine so that I can work out for myself when you have gone how to build a vessel like it."

On the face of it there did not seem to be anything particularly threatening about the plan; and in any event both Abna and the Amazon knew they could not hope to do much as things stood at present.

"Very well," the Amazon said at length, after giving Abna a glance, "we accept your proposition."

"Good! Let me make my first move as hostess, then, and ask you to dine with me."

"Do you suggest that we visit Voldas as well?" Abna demanded. "As I see it, setting foot on that world, or even bringing a space machine into its atmosphere, would undo the equilibrium you have built up."

"We will not visit that world," Amazon II said deliberately. "It is the first one to fall under my scientific powers and shall remain untouched until I am ready to use it. You say you have already viewed it through your x-ray telescope: let that suffice."

# CHAPTER ELEVEN
## MAROONED

They dined well and then towards evening set off for the airport in Amazon II's private atomicar.

It was when they had reached the field where the two *Ultra*'s lay in the glare of the setting sun that Amazon II made an observation.

"See for yourselves how absurd it is for me to want to retain my present machine when I behold the beauty and strength of yours. Look at the ridiculous comparison!"

Certainly "dignity and impudence" had never been more clearly typified. Amazon II's *Ultra* was no more than 100 feet in length and looked rather like a particularly grubby submarine. The giant *Ultra*, on the other hand, stretched across nearly the entire field and rose 200 feet into the air at the highest point, where lay the conning tower. At the rear reposed the blast-tubes, each one of them a good twenty feet in diameter.

"I shall model a new vessel like yours," Amazon II said. "Now I would like to see the interior."

"In some ways your personal lack of foresight is more than obvious," the Amazon herself remarked.

"If I were in your place I would be wary of being kidnapped and never returned to my world, thereby destroying your authority and your plans for good. No such prescience seems to possess you."

Amazon II hesitated, conscious for a brief moment perhaps that she was not really thinking for herself but using the thoughts of another.

"Kidnapping me would not destroy the plan I've worked out, for the simple reason that others would carry it on."

The effort to explain away the absence of a natural gift of foresight had a pitiful quality somehow, but neither the Amazon nor Abna pursued the point. Probably there was considerable truth in Amazon II's statement anyway.

"We are ready when you are," Abna reminded at length, and at that Amazon II broke off her study of the externals of the giant *Ultra* and stepped into the control room through the airlock. Here she gazed in fascinated interest about her.

"Help yourself," the Amazon herself invited laconically. "I very much doubt if you'll be able to assimilate all the scientific knowledge which is suggested here— not without blueprints. This design of this vessel took me many years to perfect."

"But the basis is here: that is all I need...." Amazon II began to move around, studying the layout, until Abna spoke from beside the switchboard.

"We're taking off now. You'd better lie down on one of the pressure-beds. Acceleration is severe with a ship this size."

Amazon II nodded and obeyed instructions, while the Amazon herself pressed the switch that closed the airlock. Then she, too, lay down, and Abna started up the power plant. Then the *Ultra* had swept out of the planet's atmosphere and was floating freely in the void. Immediately Abna cut the accelerative power to create Earth-norm gravity.

"Which planet first?" he inquired, as the two women stood up from the pressure-bunks.

Amazon II crossed to the window and surveyed the void with its blinding sun and six equidistant planets.

"Best policy is to start with the nearest one," she said finally, "and then visit them all in turn. That will give me plenty of time in which to watch how this machine is controlled."

Abna nodded. He felt he had the answer now to Amazon II's rather odd suggestion that a tour should be made of the hexagonal system. Presumably it was so that she could work out for herself how this giant vessel was operated, then later she could turn the information to her own use in building a better version of her present *Ultra*.

He turned the course of the vessel to the orbital path of the nearest planet, third in order from distant Voldas, and the Amazon herself came and stood beside him, contemplating the view.

"Come to think of it," the Amazon murmured, inclining her head towards Abna. "I perhaps had a good idea when I suggested we could kidnap her. We could, you know. In fact, we could go one better than that and maroon her."

Abna gave a rather troubled smile. "You sound as though you're reverting to type, Vi."

"Sorry," the Amazon sighed. "Now and again the old urge comes back on me."

"You're doing all right," Abna told her gently. "Just keep the stopper on those baser urges, that's all. Once we've got this mental parasite back to her world, we'll pull out, as she suggested, and pick up Viona on the way. We've got something here that's bigger than we can handle."

"Yes...I suppose so." The Amazon was clearly unwilling to admit the fact.

The Amazon fell silent as her double came forward again, and from that moment onwards, Amazon II kept her concentration entirely centered on Abna's control of the vessel—until at length the comparatively short hop to the nearby planet had been completed and the *Ultra* began to descend swiftly through the cloud-banks.

"Do you suggest we descend on this planet or just fly over it?" Abna questioned. "I cannot see much point in making a landing. We might descend into swamp and ooze."

"There are plenty of clear patches and rock plateaus," Amazon II replied. "I know, because I've been here before. It may surprise you, but life here is quite civilized even though the planet itself is slow to develop."

"Civilized life?" the Amazon repeated, astonished.

"Where? I don't observe any."

"You will. This planet has many odd features. Possibly you have worlds near to you which are in a similar state."

The Amazon remained silent, watching as Abna steered the *Ultra* with unerring accuracy towards a rocky plateau in the midst of the all-surrounding jungle.

The Amazon moved the airlock switch and the huge operculum swung slowly open. A warm wind, laden with the drugging perfume of flowers, or else plants, came wafting in. The planet was evidently a world of tropical jungles.

Abna moved forward and looked around him on the deserted plateau, his gun leveled. Then he jumped outside and held up his hands to catch the Amazon. She descended lithely and they turned to catch Amazon II. Instead, to their amazement, they saw the airlock door closing.

"What the—?" Abna gasped in alarm, then just as quickly he flung himself forward. But he was a second or two too late. At almost the same moment there came the familiar roar, which presaged a take-off.

"Jump, Abna!" the Amazon yelled. "You'll be carried away—"

But Abna had already foreseen this. He jumped for it even as the vessel began to quiver. In a swirl of hot air and flaming smoke it was on its way, flashing upwards toward the cloudbanks and then disappearing.

Slowly Abna got to his feet, his handsome face dark with rage. The Amazon came hurrying across to him.

"For the first time in our lives, Vi, we can write ourselves off as gullible fools," he said bitterly. "So neatly done, too! Evidently you never thought of such a trick, either?"

"Frankly, no. It's the very thing I planned to do to her. I wish to heaven I'd stuck to my idea now."

"Perhaps, somehow, she guessed your thoughts...."

The Amazon shook her head. "I don't think so. This was a planned piece of work. The whole idea of the tour was evidently to ditch us here."

Abna compressed his lips and looked at the empty, cloudy sky. "What's the use of the why and wherefore? What we've got to do is try to fathom how we get out of this one. Certainly she won't ever come back for us."

# CHAPTER TWELVE
## VIONA'S PROPOSAL

For a long time there was silence between them. They were each realizing the same thing. They had no provisions whatever, though they were well armed against attack.

"Better head for the jungles" Abna said finally. "We can see if there are any edible roots or fruits worth having. There might be, since the atmosphere here is non-poisonous."

He turned, and the Amazon fell into step beside him.

"No signs of life yet, anyway," Abna said presently. "Either wild or civilized. Once we get into this jungle we'd better rig up some kind of shelter and then think what comes next."

"I suppose," the Amazon asked, when they had gained the outskirts of the jungle, "you couldn't convey us back to the Parasite Planet by metaphysical means? You've done it on other occasions when we've been in a tight corner."

"True. Vi, but this is different. I don't doubt I could accomplish the metaphysical part, but I'd have to know exactly what the position of the Parasite Planet is in space, otherwise we might resolve into the void, with disastrous results. But we'll find a way out. Never fear."

The Amazon did not reply. For once she had an even clearer view than Abna of the danger of the present predicament.

"Wonder if these are edible?"

In the all-pervading gray light created by the sunlight filtering through the dense cloud canopy, clumps of fruit resembling oranges were visible. Experimentally, Abna tasted one and then stood reflecting.

"Sweet enough, and a bit meaty," he announced. "If it is poisonous I'll have to put myself right by mind over matter. If not, then we have a food supply of sorts."

For a while afterwards there was a strained silence, then at length Abna shrugged.

"No reaction at all. Vi. Help yourself."

She thrust her gun back in its holster and reached to the nearest clump. At the same instant an all-black sinuous shape slithered out of the tree's upper branches and coiled at lightning speed about her arm. Almost before she realized it, she was dragged from her feet.

"Abna! Quick!" she gasped.

He had moved away from the tree, but at her cry he swung back. For a split second he took in the vision of an ebony-colored python-like creature.

By this time she was several feet from the ground, relentlessly held by her updragged arm. The pressure upon it was tightening with every second until she felt the bones would snap. Nevertheless, she struggled frantically with her free hand to reach the gun in her belt—unsuccessfully.

Abna swung and maneuvered himself about, trying to find a point where he could turn his own gun on the snake and avoid hitting the Amazon. The Amazon felt she had about reached the limit of her staying power when a needle-thin blast of energy from Abna's gun darted within inches of her face.

Instantly the reptile released its grip, its fantastically long body split in two by the energy. The Amazon dropped heavily to the ground, disgustedly flinging away from her the dying half of the snake still coiled about her. Breathless, shaken, she scrambled to her feet with Abna's assistance.

"Nice playmates they've got here," he muttered. "You still in one piece, Vi?"

"Just about." She drew her sleeve over her face. "Next time I'll have sense enough to keep my gun in my hand."

Within a matter of moments she had recovered again, pulled down a clump of the fruits, and then locked about her.

"If this is a sample of the wildlife here, Abna, we're in for a lovely time. The way things are looking right now, we're going to spend the rest of our days here!"

* * * * * * *

Back on the planet Voldas, Viona had initiated herself comfortably with the governing body of the planet's major city. Everywhere she went she met with friendly courtesy and co-operation. She took up residence with Cesnon and his family, and apart from brief relaxation—when she took care to seek the company of Mexone—she spent her time using the somewhat archaic laboratories that had been placed at her disposal. Usually, the scientists of Voldas were present with her, listening to her explanations and making copious notes and designs of x-ray equipment, and then moving on to the designing of supersonic aircraft.

Curiously enough, the first thing that became evident to Viona when the first test x-ray machine was completed was the fact that the brain structure of these people of Voldas was vastly different to that of an Earthling, despite the similarity in outward physique. Viona did not know it, of course, but here—in part— lay the explanation of why these people were not mental parasites, able to pick up Earth thought-waves. They were an individual race, distinct on their own as Earthlings themselves.

"To my mind," Mexone said, as one evening he and Viona took time out to stroll, "you are quite the most wonderful person I have ever met. I don't mean that lightly, as a young man might say to the girl of his choice: I mean it with the deepest respect."

"Thanks," Viona responded, with a rather rueful smile. The last thing she wanted was "respect" in this sense. Her inward hope was that the good-looking but reserved young man would break down eventually and be human.

"Your tremendous grasp of science is so impressive," Mexone added. "Radio, astronomy, aeronautics, town planning, mathematics of the most abstruse kind. Nothing comes amiss to you. You must have an extraordinary mind."

"I have extraordinary parents, Mexone. Incidentally, I wonder how my parents are faring? They've been away a fortnight now and there's no word from them, or sign of their return."

"Word from them?" Mexone repeated, surprised. "Did you expect any?"

"I had rather hoped for a radio message, yes—. Oh, of course, I am forgetting! Space-radio is something unknown to you as yet. You'll find out about it in time: it's only radio of a very short wave variety."

"There you go again!' Mexone spread his hands. "Can you wonder that I respect you as I do?"

"Nothing more than that?" Viona asked archly, and that brought the young scientist to a stop.

"Matter, of fact there's a good deal more," he admitted, slowly beginning to move on again with the girl at his side. "I hardly dare to speak of it, though. You are a brilliant scientist and belong to a totally different world—"

"Not so totally, Mexone. Men and women of Earth look exactly like men and women here. As to my scientific knowledge, that does not stop me having the instincts of a young woman, you know."

"That," Mexone smiled, "even sounds like what you would call a proposal."

"Bluntly, it is!" Viona's eyes were perfectly frank in the fading light. "It just happens that any proposal should come from your side, not mine."

"Not here." Mexone shook his head. "Our custom has it that it is the lady who takes the lead, deciding on whatever man takes her fancy. Things always seem to work out better that way."

Viona hesitated, inwardly astonished. All of a sudden it made a lot of things clear to her.

"Mexone, does this mean that all the hints you have been giving me about myself have been to try to make me offer a proposal?"

"I got as near as I could without usurping your privilege, Viona. Since our customs are different from yours, I may as well confess that I've been in love with you from the first moment I saw you—and what I have seen of your scientific powers and generosity has only increased my regard. After which statement, if I were on your world, I suppose I'd ask you to marry me. That I cannot do: the initiative rests with you."

# CHAPTER THIRTEEN
## VIONA TAKES ACTION

Both of them had come to a stop in the lowering dark. In the distance the lights of the city had come into being: overhead loomed the fantastic sky with its awe-inspiring backdrop of the Milky Way. But neither Viona nor Mexone were conscious of these things. As on any world, anywhere, their thoughts at this moment were purely for each other.

"I cannot so easily uproot the ingrained tradition of my own world," Viona said at last, after Mexone had kissed her gently. "I just can't ask you to marry me, so I'll do the next best and accept your offer. Sounds roundabout, but it means the same thing."

"And we can't want anything more than that," Mexone laughed.

They went on again, arm-in-arm, heading now for the turn in the pathway that would finally bring them back to the city.

"I would like nothing better," Viona said, "than to stay on this world—you and I. Between us we could build up this civilization into something magnificent. I could feel the assignment was mine alone."

"Yes...." There was a queer, troubled note in Mexone's voice. "That would be wonderful, if you had not other obligations."

"What obligations?"

"Aren't you one of the three Cosmic Crusaders? Won't your parents expect you to stay beside them in their explorations? I've only just thought of it, but it seems to me that your life is dedicated to your noble cause, not to marrying one man like me and settling down on one planet."

Viona laughed. "My parents will make no demands on me, I promise you. They would like to have me with them, no doubt, but they will just as graciously let me go my own way."

"Well, that's a relief!" Mexone exclaimed, brightening. "Let's get back to my family and tell them the good news!"

They discovered, however, when they arrived back at Mexone's home that, though the news of their engagement was accepted joyfully enough, there was a certain air of worry about Cesnon's manner—almost an agitation.

"A special messenger was sent to find you, Viona."

"Oh?" She waited interestedly. "Something gone wrong with the scientific experiments?"

"Much worse, my dear. The scientists have noticed that creeping paralysis is returning!"

Viona's expression changed and she turned for the door. "This can't wait another moment! Come with me, Mexone: I'll need you as interpreter."

Their own affairs forgotten, they wasted no time in reaching the headquarters of the city's scientific control. She hurried straight to the office of the governing director, Mexone close behind her. The gravity of the director's face as he rose to meet them was more than obvious.

"Quickly!" Viona made an impatient movement. "Get the facts from him, Mexone."

Mexone did so and Viona waited in exasperation at the exchange of the alien language; then at last Mexone turned to her.

"No doubt about it, Viona. The same effects as before. Clocks are commencing to run slow; parts of our planet are having abnormally cold weather, and also in those cold regions the people are complaining of a form of cramp. Everything fits in: the 'freezing' process has begun again."

"According to my parents," Viona said at length to Mexone, who would have to make the interpretation afterwards, "the cause of the thermo-equilibrium is that planet nearest your sun. There are two answers: either my parents guessed wrong and that inner world is not responsible; or else something has happened to my parents and they are powerless to stop the machinations of the people of the inner world. Our first move has to be to make sure that the inner world is responsible."

"And how do we do that?" Mexone asked.

"By building a detector. Since this thermo-equilibrium is artificially produced, the radiation or whatever it is causing it, will reveal itself on a detector. It won't take long to rig one up. Translate that back to the director, will you?"

Mexone did so quickly, and during this time Viona was already at work sketching a design of the instrument she had in mind. From then on there was no more delay.

Once completed, the detector was set up in the main laboratory and a current passed through it. In grim silence, Viona, Mexone, the director, and attendant scientists watched the needle swing instantly and maintain a fixed position. Viona calculated quickly and then checked her figures with the one computer that the laboratory possessed. With this final checking went the last shred of doubt.

"Definitely caused by the inner world," she announced, and Mexone translated quickly.

"Then how do we stop it?" Mexone asked anxiously.

"That I don't know," Viona replied, her brow troubled. "I have a good scientific knowledge, as you're aware, but there sometimes appear problems beyond my handling. The only ones who can neutralize this trouble are my parents. And that is what is puzzling me: why they haven't done something to prevent this happening? Why they've never communicated."

There was an anxious silence for a moment or two, then the director said something which Mexone quickly translated.

"In three weeks, Viona, or even less, we'll be back in a state of paralysis."

"Only one thing for it," Viona decided. "Somehow I have got to get in touch with my parents and have them go to work on this business immediately...." The terrible thought occurred to her that perhaps her parents were dead, then she brushed it quickly from her mind.

"And how do we get in touch with them?" Mexone asked, and Viona tried not to look irritable.

"By radio—space radio, which is the only possible answer at this stage. We'll have to convert one of the ordinary radio transmitters for the purpose. It won't take more than a couple of hours."

Tireless, completely ignoring the fact that she had spent the whole night in intense concentration, Viona went to work on her next task—which lay in the radio transmission rooms adjoining the main laboratory.

"Anywhere near finished?" Mexone asked, when gray daylight was commencing to pale the windows.

"Just about." Viona checked over the details of the modified transmitter.

She placed her finger on one of the main leads and Mexone watched in surprise as he noticed that in her other hand she held a voltmeter. A tremendous surge of current, nearly up to 10,000 volts, registered itself.

"Are you passing that terrific current through yourself?" he asked in amazement, and Viona nodded briefly as she removed her finger from the lead.

"Yes, I think we're ready to try," she said, and Mexone translated as usual; then she settled herself before the instrument, switched on, and drew the microphone to her. In the speaker there came a crackling of violent static. Viona touched a button and the static abated somewhat.

"Violent interference," she said, seeing Mexone's glance. "I don't think it will be severe enough to prevent an answer being received, though."

"Your parents have radio with them?" Mexone questioned.

"They have both the radio equipment of the *Ultra*, and also wrist-radio for portable use."

More adjustments; then Viona spoke into the microphone.

"Viona calling mother and father—Amazon and Abna," Viona repeated, but there still was no response. She waited for at least ten minutes, at the end of which time she was compelled to admit defeat.

"It begins to look—" Mexone commenced slowly, but Viona cut him short.

"I know perfectly well how it looks—that some mishap has befallen my mother and father. The only other solution is that the sun being so close to that inner planet, it prevents radio reception or transmission." Viona got to her feet and sighed with genuine weariness. "Our only chance now is to visit the inner world and see what can be done to either stop this process of thermo-equilibrium, or else arrive at some compromise."

"You've no space machine," Mexone pointed out.

"I shall have—within four or five days if the scientists will stand by me. A small one capable of making the journey can be built in that time. Once I reach the inner world, I can perhaps do something. At the very least I may discover what has happened to my mother and father."

"You speak as though you intend to go alone, Viona. I'm going with you—not only to offer as much help as I can, but also because I wish to find out what space travel is like."

Viona smiled tiredly. "I'm glad to hear you say that. That I'll be happier with company goes without saying. You'd better tell the scientists what I've decided to do, then the moment we have had a meal and a rest we'll get to work...."

# CHAPTER FOURTEEN
## RENDEZVOUS IN SPACE

Viona was wrong in thinking that perhaps her radio message had not been received. It had, in detail, by Amazon II, and its contents caused her a good deal of surprise. In silence she studied it in the main radio-reception headquarters in "London," to which point the message had been sent.

"And this came through an hour ago?" she inquired at length.

"Yes, Amazon. You had not been back very long from your space journey. I thought you ought to know at once."

"Yes, indeed.... This is a very intriguing message—especially the second one, which refers so blandly to 'mother and father.' I trust you grasp the significance of that?"

"I can only assume, Amazon, that the two usurpers who came here did not tell you their entire story. They must have a daughter—since the message was in a woman's voice—who is resident on Voldas."

"That appears to be it," Amazon II acknowledged, thinking. "And those two whom I've marooned on

Jaxa—the hell planet—were not usurpers, my friend. I think their story of coming from a world called Earth was true, and I also believe that the thoughts I have were once those of the original Amazon. But they certainly did not refer to their daughter, who is evidently another member of this fantastic 'Cosmic Crusaders' group. It will be interesting to see what the daughter does. I want a watch kept on Voldas night and day. If a spaceship leaves that planet, inform me. In its present state of Voldas' civilization space travel is unknown, so if it takes place we can be sure that the daughter is responsible for it. I'll deal with her quickly enough if the occasion demands it."

"A watch is already being kept on Voldas, Amazon, to be sure that all goes well with the paralysis process."

"Yes, of course. I had forgotten that. Just keep me informed of whatever happens."

\* \* \* \* \* \* \*

And on Voldas, once the time for eating and resting were over, Viona went back to work, this time supervising the construction of a small space machine, just large enough to hold Mexone and herself in its crude control room, and powered by a small atomic plant similar to that used in the giant *Ultra*. Apprehension as to the fate of her parents, and the obvious slowing down of Voldas' molecular processes gave Viona a demoniac energy that surprised even herself. She allowed herself, and those helping her, only the very minimum of spare time for rest and refreshment, but there were no grumbles since it was realized that the sands were running out.

Altogether, it took Viona, Mexone, and the scientists two weeks to complete the tiny space machine. Once it was tested and proved spaceworthy, Viona wasted no more time. She paid her respects to the head of the governing body, made no promises, and thereupon took off from the planet with Mexone as her only companion. They had considerable supplies of provisions and all the weapons Viona deemed necessary: beyond this they would have to rely on their own ingenuity.

To Mexone, the wonders of space were fascinating, seeing them as he was for the first time. To Viona the void was no longer impressive, so she spent her time at the controls while Mexone surveyed the deeps, made copious notes, and took endless photographs and lengths of movie film.

They were an hour out from Voldas with that world lying to their left now as a mighty globe edged with stars, when Mexone came back somewhat to realities.

"How long will this journey to the inner world take, Viona? And incidentally, where is it? I still can't see it."

"As to time—maybe five more hours," Viona replied. "This ship hasn't the terrific power of the *Ultra*, remember. As for the inner world itself, it lies there, to the left of the sun; if you drop the dark shades you'll see it."

Mexone pressed a switch and dense light-neutralizing shields fell across the small observation port. In silence he watched the imperceptibly growing planet that lay close to the sun of this sun.

It was half an hour later, when Viona was again checking the course and studying the now bigger disk, that she became aware of the unusual. There was a pinpoint object between herself and the planet, catching the light of the off-side sun.

"What is it?" Mexone asked, puzzled, coming to her side.

"With the naked eye it looks like a space ship. But I've learned never to trust the naked eye." Viona moved to the small telescope and adjusted the lenses; then she gave a little whistle of delighted surprise. "Not only a space ship, but the *Ultra*!" she cried. "My parents must be on the return trip, or something! Oh, thank heaven! I was beginning to fear the worst. Here, take a look. I'll get in touch with them by radio."

Mexone peered through the eyepiece and Viona moved quickly to the radio equipment. In a matter of seconds she had the instrument transmitting.

"Viona calling. Have just sighted your vessel. Confirm that you are both safe. Over."

Almost immediately the answer came. "Hello, Viona! A good job you identified yourself. That vessel of yours is certainly a patched-up looking job." It was definitely the voice of the Golden Amazon, and yet there was a peculiar brittle quality about it which Viona found hard to understand. Then she decided it must be the fault of the hastily contrived radio equipment. And the voice of Amazon II continued: "I'm alone in the *Ultra*, Viona. Your father has stayed behind to try and settle one or two scientific problems."

"There's only one scientific problem at the moment, mother—the return of thermo-equilibrium to—"

"Yes, Viona, I know. We will discuss that when we meet. I will bring the *Ultra* alongside as soon as we're near enough and anchor your vessel with the magnetic grapples."

"Right," Viona responded. "See you later."

She switched off and stood in thought for a moment or two. Mexone came slowly to her side.

"Anything the matter, Viona?"

"Naturally I'm glad my parents are safe...." Viona gave an odd glance. "I just don't quite understand why mother seems so indifferent to this thermo-equilibrium problem." She shrugged. "Well, maybe she has her reasons."

She turned back to the switchboard and set about the task of slowing the machine's velocity, timing it so that when the mighty bulk of the *Ultra* finally came level she was able swiftly to turn the little vessel around and head it in the same direction as the giant. In this manner they came alongside each other and the magnetic grapples did the rest. From airlock to airlock a sealed bellows-passage was projected, making it possible for Viona and Mexone to cross from one ship to the other without need of space suits.

Amazon II looked vaguely surprised as the two came into the control-room. Her eyes went beyond Viona to

Mexone; then she closed the switch that withdrew the bellows-passage and cut off the power of the attractors. Outside, the little space ship, ejected beyond the grip of the giant *Ultra*'s magnetic field, began to drift away lazily into space.

The Amazon II forced a smile and held out her hand. "Nice to see you again, Viona, and I got your radio message sent out from Voldas."

"Voldas?" Viona repeated. "Oh, is that what Mexone's world is called?"

"By the people of the inner planet, yes. Those on Voldas will have their own name for their planet, of course."

Amazon II's gaze strayed back again to Mexone. At least she had learned his name, but she was not aware of his attachment to Viona.

"Just why didn't you answer my radio call?" Viona asked, puzzled. "You must have realized what I wanted to talk about. The return of the paralysis—"

"That is not going to be an easy problem to overcome, Viona," Amazon II said quietly. "The people of the inner world are highly organized, scientific, and efficient. They have an immense campaign in hand for the eventual control of this entire hexagonal system. At the time of your radio call your father and I were unable to get at the *Ultra*, where lay the only apparatus for sending back a message to you. In any case, even had the sending of a message been possible, we would hardly have dared to send it. It would have been picked up."

"Oh...I see." There was an awkward silence as Viona apparently thought something out for herself. "And yet you managed to get to the *Ultra* eventually? Must have, since you're here aboard it."

"Eventually, yes—by taking the most fantastic risk. Even at that I was only just able to manage it. Your father had to stay behind. He has a plan in mind for defeating these scientists of the inner world. I, for my part, was heading to Voldas to find you. I thought that between us we could work on the problem better by counteracting the thermo-equilibrium effect on Voldas itself."

"In that case, hadn't we better turn back to Voldas and carry out your plan?" Mexone asked, but the second Amazon shook her head.

"No. I've been studying Voldas through the telescope and I see now that the paralytic process is too far advanced for us to do anything on Voldas itself. Since you are both here, you had better come back with me to the inner world and we'll work on the problem along with your father."

Viona nodded and turned away thoughtfully. Amazon II eyed her for a moment, then moved to the control board and slowly turned the *Ultra*'s huge bulk around so that the vessel headed back in the direction of the inner world. As this turning-about maneuver took place Viona had one glimpse of her abandoned space ship. It was drifting toward the field of the nearest gravitational body—not the sun or inner world, since they were still far away—but the closer attraction of

Jaxa, the hell planet.

"Is there something the matter?" Mexone asked in a low voice, as he reached Viona's side. "There's a sort of mystified look on your face."

Viona did not answer, but she gave a warning look. Under the pretext of gazing through the window, her back to the Amazon II, she withdrew from her tunic belt a small object like a compass and depressed the sapphire-topped button on its side. Instantly the small needle swung to a zero mark and remained there. Viona's eyes became hard as she studied it.

"What?" Mexone murmured.

"This woman," Viona answered, under her breath, "Is not my mother! This is an aura-compass I'm holding, its purpose being for the needle to swing to a given number, the number being the periodicity of the energy-aura emanated by any living being. No two are alike. I've switched this to the number corresponding to my mother's aura and you see what happens! The needle swings to zero instead of to the number."

"What, then, are you going to do? Where is your mother?"

"I haven't the slightest idea—but one thing I do know. We have got to defeat this twin of my mother's before she defeats us."

# CHAPTER FIFTEEN
## THE AMAZON FIGHTS

In the jungle depths of Jaxa, the hell planet, the Amazon and Abna still lived, though both of them were wondering how much longer they were going to hold out.

"Funny thing," the Amazon mused. "We've faced death innumerable times in the past and always escaped—death in far more fantastic forms than faces us here, and yet it begins very much to look as though we're going to end our careers in the most unspectacular way possible—as fodder for dinosaurs!"

Abna, sprawled on a bed of giant leaves, gave a shrug.

"Before I'll sacrifice myself to any monster I'll make a blind stab at mind-over-matter transportation back to the inner world. If I miss—as I probably shall—and we die in the void, it'll be preferable to being the prey of a monster, anyway."

"If only we'd thought to strap on our wrist-radios," the Amazon said bitterly, at length. "We might have contacted Viona and found some way out of this."

"Useless regret, Vi. We were as innocent as children

when we stepped out of the *Ultra*, never guessing for a moment that things would work out the way they did."

Outside, the view was unchanged. The mighty primeval forest, deadly silent, lighted by the gray glow that passed for daylight.

"Food supply is running pretty low if you feel like doing anything about it," Abna remarked, getting to his feet. "One of us must stay here and protect the shelter against attack."

The Amazon glanced back over her shoulder. "I'll get some fruits. It's my turn, anyway."

She stepped outside, gun in hand, and made her way with lithe movements through the waist-high bushes and gigantic, headily-perfumed flowers. She failed to catch sight of—or even hear, since the beast was down-wind to her—a monstrous cat-like animal, somewhat similar to a terrestrial tiger of the sabertooth variety. It was far bigger than anything ever born on Earth, even in prehistoric times—a magnificent beast with a tawny, satin-smooth coat, and emerald-green eyes. As it moved, its upper lip quivered back from the huge saber tusks in its upper jaw.

Immediately her back was turned the 'tiger' sprang. It misjudged the distance and dropped three feet from her, to prepare for its second leap. Instantly the Amazon swung, aimed her gun, and pressed the discharging button. To her horror no searing pencil of energy flashed forth: there was only a faint buzzing, the sound made when the cheap diamonds used for energy had become exhausted.

The brute sprang again, flying through the air with teeth bared to the limit and claws extended like grappling hooks. The Amazon did not run: that would have been fatal. Instead she coldly calculated the distance even as the animal shot toward her—then with a tremendous dive she torpedoed herself underneath its body, staggering up behind it as it dropped.

If it were possible for an animal to look bewildered, this one looked it at that moment. Never before had a prey escaped by diving beneath it. With a scream of rage it twirled round, its tail smashing down the shrubbery with furious lashings, and in those split seconds the Amazon started to run, heading towards what she hoped was the blazed trail back to the shelter. In a very short time she found she was wrong—and completely lost. Running at top speed she came into a clearing, looked frantically about her, then dashed on again. To the rear was the smashing of branches and twigs as the 'tiger' followed her up.

Again the beast sprang, jaws distended. With all the power of her arm the Amazon snatched up a nearby branch, and slammed it home, straight between the awful teeth and down into the beast's cavernous mouth and gullet. It gasped and choked with the pain, reared up in the air, and then began to claw frantically at its mouth as a cat might in trying to extract a bone.

The Amazon began to withdraw warily, without turning her back—when suddenly, to her alarm, the branch became dislodged. With a final mighty rip of its claw the tiger ripped the obstruction free and, bleeding freely from the mouth and more incensed than ever, it charged in unholy fury for this nimble and deadly enemy.

This time there was no dead branch handy, no time to run. The Amazon went down before the brute's onrush, only just missing having those awful claws tear her open to the bones of her chest. Flat on her back, her legs scissored round the brute's haunches, she thrust her relentless hands under its jaw, thus keeping the saber fangs away from her sweat-drenched face.

She pushed even harder, straining her superb strength to its uttermost limit, and powerful though the animal was, it began to whimper with pain at the frightful strain being imposed on its spine, the girl's legs pinning its rear so it could not move.

The beast reared suddenly, its ears alert, its whole attention gone from her. It actually seemed to cringe as its huge green eyes stared skywards—then, some desperate animal fear in its mind, it suddenly called off the attack and raced into the jungle with its tail drooping in fright.

Too exhausted to understand the mystery, the Amazon just lay as she was for a moment or two; then she too heard something, a something that must have become apparent much sooner to the keener hearing of the animal. It was a high-pitched scream from the sky, becoming louder and louder until it sent up ear-shattering echoes throughout the jungle silence.

Alarmed herself now, the Amazon got to her feet and stared about her. The scream reached a point when she felt her eardrums would split under its intensity, when it suddenly vanished in a tremendous concussion that made the ground quiver momentarily. The silence returned, heavy after the awe-inspiring din.

She had a pretty good idea of where the object had fallen, but she also had to remember that she had no gun with her, and there was no guarantee but what she would again be attacked. On the other hand, she had also lost the trail back to the shelter, so in either direction she would have to take a big risk. After a second or two she made up her mind and began moving in the direction where she believed the object had fallen. She had only covered perhaps a dozen yards, however, when to her relief she heard her name being called.

# CHAPTER SIXTEEN
## ESCAPE

"Vi! Vi, where are you? Can you hear me?"

"Here, Abna!" she shouted, making a megaphone of her hands. "On your left!"

She had to call again several times and give her direction before at last Abna came plunging into view through the dense undergrowth, his gun at the ready in his hand.

"Thank goodness to see you—and a gun," the Amazon exclaimed, as he joined her. "I've been enjoying myself no end."

"What kept you?" he asked, puzzled. "I became anxious when you didn't return, so thought I'd better investigate. I found signs of a scuffle near the fruit tree outcropping—"

"Scuffle is right!" Briefly the Amazon explained what had happened and Abna stood looking at her seriously.

"Thank heaven you're all right, anyway," he said at last, "You heard that scream, then? Of course you must have done since it scared away the sabertooth."

"I'm on my way now to find out what it was. I've

got the rather crazy hope that it might be a space machine—perhaps my double regretting her action, though I'm afraid there isn't much chance of it."

They neither of them wasted any more time. Both were convinced that they were moving in the right direction, so notching the trees as they went, they pushed through the vines and bushes until, abruptly, they came upon the object they were seeking. They stopped, almost unable to credit the miraculous nature of the vision.

Lying amidst the tree branches and vegetation which it had brought down in its plunge was a space machine, upended, of extremely crude design. From it an intense heat was still radiating after its frictional passage through the atmosphere, but as far as the two could see—for they dared not go too near to it—it was only superficially damaged. A plate or two buckled in the nose seemed to be worst trouble. In the main, the soft, wet loam of the forest had prevented any really violent impact. And around the tilted vessel the vegetation was scorched and withered, but thanks to its general wetness no forest fire had developed.

"Well," Abna said at length, "I don't know where it came from, but if it's at all spaceworthy it's all we need. Since it won't be cool enough to examine for some hours yet we'd better return to the shelter and collect some fruit on the way. Then we'll come back."

Plainly this was the most sensible plan, and they followed it out, not encountering any more jungle beasts in the process. Both of them were wondering in perplexity where the spaceship had come from—one so crude and obviously "thrown together." Naturally they had no means of knowing it was Viona's abandoned vessel which had dropped into the attraction of Jaxa and thus been irresistibly drawn towards it.

"A guided missile, perhaps?" Abna suggested at length, but the Amazon looked dubious.

"Could be—but somehow I doubt it. There's something very strange about this whole business."

Towards evening they set out for the ship.

Still deeply puzzled, the Amazon and Abna entered the control room and looked around them. At a touch on a switch the lights came up, so evidently the batteries were still in good order.

"All very queer," Abna said presently. "On the face of it, it looks as though the pilot of this machine leapt into space and left the door open behind him. Wonder why?"

"Conjectures don't matter anyway," the Amazon told him, studying the power plant. "We have here a serviceable power plant, and fortunately it was switched off before the mystery happened, so hardly any atomic fuel has been used. There is more than enough here to carry us back to the inner world, or even the world where we left Viona."

Abna crossed to the Amazon's side and examined the power plant carefully; then he looked up with a puzzled frown.

"Notice something here, Vi?" he asked. "This power plant and the general method of wiring-distribution, is almost identical with our own system! Only one person besides us knows of the system, and that's Viona."

"Yes, you're right!" The Amazon made the admission in surprise; then her expression changed. "If Viona was the pilot of this machine and has met her death through any machinations on the part of that mental parasite who's imitating me, I'll blast that inner planet apart! I'll tear—"

"We don't know anything yet, for certain," Abna reminded her quietly. "Time enough to think about reprisal when we know the facts. Better make a routine checkup and see if this thing is spaceworthy."

They did so, and at the end of half an hour decided that it was. The front plates, though severely dented, were still airtight, and the rest of the vessel seemed to be in reasonably good shape.

"That settles it then," Abna said. "Nothing to do but take off and head for the planet where we left Viona. Once we know the real facts we can get busy."

Abna closed the power circuit and immediately the power plant responded, sending the little vessel hurtling into the void, away from the hell-world of monsters.

# CHAPTER SEVENTEEN
## AMAZON II VERSUS VIONA

Aboard the *Ultra*, the inner world—or Diaboli, as Viona had so aptly christened it—was drawing near. So near indeed, that Viona realized it was time for action on her part. Once on that inner world she would have little chance of defeating this creature who was masquerading as her mother. She had to be overcome now, after which some kind of plan could be worked out....

And, so far, Amazon II had no suspicion that her spurious identity had been betrayed to the aura-detector. She imagined Viona and Mexone were merely discussing the view outside when she noticed them deep in conversation. It therefore came as a complete surprise to her when, in turning from the switchboard, she found herself looking straight into the muzzle of Viona's leveled proton-gun.

"And what is the reason for this?" she asked deliberately, moving slowly forward. "First time I've ever known you to turn on your own mother, Viona."

"I have never turned on my mother, and never shall. You are not my mother. You resemble her—but that's all. In a dozen ways you have given yourself away."

"You're being ridiculous, child! What notion has—"

"Let me finish speaking," Viona commanded, advancing a little and watching keenly for any lightning moves.

"You can save your breath trying to defend your identity. I want the facts. Where are my mother and father and what are you doing in complete control of their spaceship?"

Amazon II hesitated, then: "Your parents are on my own world, whither we are now bound. You'd be well advised not to use that gun on me, otherwise you'll never find your parents. I'm the only one who knows where they are."

"You don't scare me with that threat," Viona retorted. "If I think you're an enemy, I'll dispose of you and risk finding my mother and father. I don't want to kill deliberately because that is not my policy, but I'm taking over control of this vessel from here on, and Mexone has a second gun to cover you. Get away from that switchboard!"

Amazon II did not move. Instead she said: "Very well, I admit that I am not your mother: you can't blame me for attempting the deception. My plan was to take you to my home planet, give you every freedom, and at the same tune have you work beside me in the consummation of a plan for the rulership of this particular system. I should have thought that would have appealed to you."

"Then you couldn't be more wrong! I'm not interested in plans for the rulership of other worlds, which are probably quite content as they are. And what of Mexone here? What had you planned for him?"

"The commandership of his own planet, Voldas, when I decide to take it over."

"From which I assume that you admit responsibility for the condition of thermo-equilibrium which is again threatening it?"

"Certainly I do. Since it has not the scientific ingenuity to save itself, it must fall before my superior knowledge.... And you? What was your aim in crossing space?"

"To find my parents, and have them stop the very process which you have restarted. I am asking you again: where are my mother and father?"

"Dead," Amazon II replied cynically. "Or if not that, they soon will be."

"To just state that they are dead does not satisfy me. How did they die?"

"I marooned them on the one undeveloped planet in this system—a hell-world, so overridden with giant, ferocious beasts that they cannot possibly have survived!"

"I see...."

Viona was silent for a moment or two, the venom in her face typical of that of her mother when aroused. Behind her, Mexone stood somewhat uncertainly, the second gun in his hand—then, with an abruptness that was bewilderingly fast, Amazon II sprang to life from her apparently indolent position. In one leap she had reached Viona's side. The grip of her fingers and the strength of her arm had whipped the gun from Viona's grasp before she had time to even aim it.

But, though she realized in that instant that this double of her mother also had her stupendous strength, Viona was not by any means lacking when it came to muscular power. The instant the gun was snatched from her hand she slammed up the other one, bunched into a fist, and struck Amazon II a shattering blow under the jaw. Dazed, but still holding the gun, Amazon II toppled backwards but was saved from falling by the switchboard behind her.

Viona swung, intending to take the remaining gun from the astonished Mexone—who was awe-stricken, apparently, by the sight of two women of such immense muscular capabilities—but before she could do so Amazon II was upon her again, unable to use the gun at short range.

Viona landed on her face, and remembered a favorite trick of her mother's. The instant Amazon II landed on her back to continue the attack, Viona brought her arms upwards and backwards behind her head until her fingers had interlocked over Amazon II's neck from behind. It meant her head was completely imprisoned, and savagely though she fought she failed to dislodge it. Viona grinned bitterly to herself and dragged downwards with awful power, knowing full well that eventually Amazon II's neck would snap under the pressure.

Amazon II knew it as well. Accordingly she edged her bended knees slowly backwards until they had reached the small of Viona's back. Then, locking her own hands under Viona's body, she began to crush downwards with the relentless power of a hydraulic press. Viona winced, then her face twisted in pain as she could feel her backbone and organs tightening inexorably under the counter grip. Her own hold on the back of Amazon II's neck inevitably slackened, the pain being too intense for her to maintain the muscular effort. In a matter of seconds she had to release her hold and became limp, utterly exhausted. She waited for what she assumed would be the final attack to finish her,

The watching Mexone, finally provoked to reckless action by Viona's suffering, suddenly leapt forward, intent on attacking Amazon II. Instantly the superwoman lashed out a backhanded blow that struck him full in the face, sending him spinning across the control room. He tripped and collapsed, completely knocked out.

Amazon II's gaze shifted back to Viona. "Get up—and quickly!" she commanded.

Viona obeyed, but certainly not quickly. Swaying, every bone in her body aching, she stood looking at the gun trained upon her.

"I am not going to kill you just yet—or this companion of yours," Amazon II explained, glancing across to where a groaning Mexone was struggling back to consciousness. "There is a good deal of information both of you can give me before I decide to dispose of you. You, Viona, can tell me much concerning the scientific arts of your mother, and Mexone can tell me one or two facts about his planet.... Our journey has almost ended. Once on my planet I will deal with you again. Now sit over there and recover yourself. One false move and I'll forego my hope of extracting information from you and shoot you dead instead."

# CHAPTER EIGHTEEN
## MENTAL TORTURE

There was, of course, no possible chance of Abna and the Amazon, aboard their tiny space machine, seeing the *Ultra* as it descended toward the inner world. It was far, far too distant from where Jaxa lay, and, in any case neither the Amazon nor Abna were looking for it: their attention was mainly concentrated upon the world where they had left Viona in charge. And very changed this world had become. It revealed its surface occasionally as clouds mysteriously parted and then seemed to coalesce again, and that surface was grimly changed. It was gray, stone-like, and apparently had no movement upon it.

"Apparently," Abna said at length, "your double has refrozen this world. No more than we should have expected, I suppose. And presumably, if she's still there, Viona will be paralyzed along with the rest of them."

The Amazon nodded silently. There was no doubt that the planet was very close once again to thermo-dynamic equilibrium. Since Viona's departure, the process had spread and intensified at a tremendous speed, and now the only movement that remained was in the slowly decreasing air currents that caused the spasmodic cloud movements.

"One thing about it," Abna said at length, "our return there will undo the process for the second time. Your double is just going to love repeating the performance time and again."

The Amazon was too inwardly troubled to speak. Hard though her exterior manner usually was, she had a real devotion to Viona, the only living being she really cared about—with the exception of Abna. Yet even he had not first place in her affections, chiefly because of his unwitting tendency to dominate her.

"The best thing to do," the Amazon said at length, "is land as near to Cesnon's home as possible and then wait for this paralysis to cancel itself out, as it did before when we'd been on the planet about thirty minutes. Inside the ship we're not so liable to become involved in that reactionary explosion which occurs when things start moving again."

"Best idea," Abna agreed, and returned to the small switchboard to guide the little machine downwards. And it was as they came below the clouds that they noticed the view was just the same as on the first arrival: petrifaction and grayness were everywhere, but this, of course, did not prevent the identification of various landmarks.

In a matter of ten minutes Abna brought the vessel down to a gentle standstill no more than a quarter of a mile from the home of Cesnon. Silence—utter silence—fell as the power plant ceased operating; then the Amazon joined Abna at the port and gazed outside. Grayness and the settling dust, and not a thing moving anywhere—but not for long. Around the vessel there presently began to stir an immense and growing agitation, the product of a random element introduced into absolute equilibrium.

Then came the violent explosion and thunderclap; then, in an ever-widening circle from the space ship, the collapse of the frozen condition became visible. The grayness began to disperse, the dust moved in the rising wind; the gray faces of the nearby buildings began to smear and evaporate to reveal their actual nature and color below. In fifeen minutes, or less, the widening arc of "thaw" had advanced far enough to encompass the home of Cesnon.

"We can risk it now," Abna said briefly. "Let's go."

He opened the airlock and led the way outside, the Amazon close behind him. Before long they had reached the front door of Cesnon's house, but there was no response to their pounding upon the door. Abna wasted no more time. He leveled his gun at the lock and the shaft of needle-thin flame instantly ate through it. A kick, and the door was swinging wide.

"Try the lounge," the Amazon said—and her guess was right. On the lounge floor, Cesnon himself, his wife, and the young girl Adza were just struggling back to consciousness, a process which became rapidly accelerated under the tablets which Abna forced down each throat. One by one the three were heaved into chairs where they sat dazedly trying to piece things together.

"You're all right now," the Amazon said, addressing Cesnon, since he was the only one who understood the language. "It's the same old equilibrium process at work—or maybe you've realized that by now?"

Cesnon gave a slow nod, his mind clearing at last. "It—it caught up on us suddenly, even though we'd seen it coming for some days. I have a remembrance of falling, and then...."

"Where's Viona?" the Amazon cut in urgently. "That's our prime worry. Isn't she with you?"

"No. When we first saw that this equilibrium trouble was returning, she was summoned by the scientists to make suggestions for combating it. She said the problem was beyond her and that only you and Abna could deal with it. So she constructed a space ship as quickly as possible and set off with Mexone for the inner world. We haven't heard anything from her since."

"With Mexone?" Abna repeated, surprised, and Cesnon smiled.

"After you left, he and Viona became engaged."

The Amazon hardly appeared to be listening: she was lost in thought.

"So they set off for the inner world and later, by sheer chance, their spaceship fell empty on to the world of Jaxa.... Now what happened in the meantime?"

"Their—their space ship did what?" Cesnon exclaimed in alarm, rising.

The Amazon gave him the facts, which explained

sufficiently how she and Abna came to be here—but Cesnon's distress at the possible fate of his son was obvious.

"Something disastrous must have happened to them!" he exclaimed, when he had translated the details to his wife and daughter. "Amazon, what do you intend to do?"

"The only thing we can do—set off for the inner world and get the facts from there. There are a host of things that need explaining to you, Cesnon, particularly concerning the weird, mentally parasitic people who inhabit the inner world, but I just haven't got the time now. Abna and I have got to move fast, and we're going to take a pretty hefty gamble, too, since we'll probably be observed and destroyed before we can even reach the inner world. That is something we must risk. In the meantime, I don't think you need to worry about your planet. The process of returning to normal will continue for some time, and once we get to the inner world—if we ever do—we'll stop all chance of paralysis happening for the third time. Come, Abna, we've much to do."

\* \* \* \* \* \* \*

Once the return to the inner world was completed, neither Viona nor Mexone had the slightest chance of evading Amazon II's captivity. They were taken immediately to her headquarters, and though Viona could not help but notice the similarity of everybody to Earth people, the fact that this particular London was set in an earlier era of Earth had no meaning for her, since at that time she had not been born. The only person whom she might have recognized in younger form—Chris Wilson—did not appear, so she learned little of the mystery of the duality between her mother and this second Amazon. As for Mexone, he seemed completely bewildered, this excursion into scientific realms being something far beyond his normal grasp of logical things.

The only thing he did understand quite plainly were the statements of the second Amazon, and about these statements there was no doubt whatever.

The second Amazon spoke. "I said in space that before I dispose of the pair of you I mean to find out a lot of information—and I still say that. I will start with you, Viona. Your mother has a knowledge of many scientific things about which I know virtually nothing. So has your father. What are you prepared to tell me?"

"Nothing," Viona replied calmly. "In any event, you'll kill me in the finish, so I may as well die leaving you in ignorance of the secrets of many wonders."

"Evasion, and nothing else but," Amazon II retorted. "It is not that you cannot tell me: you just prefer to be obstinate. Maybe I can loosen your tongue."

Viona said nothing. Amazon II strode forward and pushed her backwards roughly until she suddenly collided with a tall, upright cabinet. The instant she did so, metallic clamps shot out and imprisoned her body in an immovable grip. With a click the clamps locked themselves and held her rigid.

"Now...." Amazon II smiled coldly as she depressed a switch. "We shall see."

At first Viona felt nothing, then after a few seconds she was aware of a strange sensation stealing over her. The laboratory and its fittings seemed to be receding at a tremendous speed while she herself was dropping into fathomless, never-ending pit. It was a falling-dream extended interminably. It was a drop in a lift-shaft that had no bottom. It was mental hell, and the slow breakage of all traces of nervous control.

Faster she dropped downwards, and faster still, apparently turning head-over-heels in the process, yet never touching the bottom of the black abyss. And out of this terrifying, ceaseless nightmare came Amazon II's pitiless voice.

"What you are experiencing, Viona, is induced terror, caused by electronic surges passing through your brain and producing a make-believe experience. The process is so designed that you will endure this terrible sensation without ceasing until you choose to show some common sense. The force is so balanced that you cannot die of heart-failure or nervous collapse. You will just endure, and endure, until you can stand it no longer...."

Viona could not answer because she was still falling and reeling into nothingness, her inside racked and strained by the eternal drop. To Mexone and Amazon II she still appeared unconscious, clamped to the machine, but the ghastly expression on her face was sufficient indication of the mental torture she was experiencing.

Then, gradually, it seemed to dawn on the slow-moving Mexone what was taking place. He shifted his gaze from Viona's imprisoned figure and stared at the Amazon II's back as she operated the switchboard.

Abruptly Mexone sprang to life, hurtled across the laboratory, and seized Amazon II under the chin from behind. A second later he realized how wrong a move he'd made. Amazon II twirled around, dislodged his grip, then lifted him up bodily over her head and flung him a dozen yards away. He crashed to the floor half-conscious, wishing he had not been such a fool as to again try conclusions with a superwoman.

At the sound of a switch clicking he raised his head. Also at that instant Viona found herself drifting back to awareness.

"Well?" Amazon II inquired coldly. "Do you wish this to go on indefinitely, or will you give me information?"

Viona looked at her dully. "I have already told you: I know nothing of the scientific miracles performed by my parents. And even if I did, I wouldn't reveal them—certainly not to one such as you."

Amazon II was silent for a long time, then she sighed.

"Very well. Obviously I am wasting my time, so there is nothing left but to dispose of you." She crossed over to Mexone and yanked him to his feet.

"As for this spineless idiot here, I don't suppose he could tell me much about his planet anyway that I don't already know. My time's precious, and the sooner I'm rid of the pair of you, the better."

Mexone did not attempt to struggle, knowing it was useless against such a woman as this. He gave Viona a helpless look and she gave a faint smile in return as it occurred to her that evidently he had made an effort to save her and got the worst of it.

Turning abruptly, Amazon II bundled Mexone across to a gigantic instrument dominated by anode and cathode globes. Between them was a grating, standing about a foot from the floor, and backed by a tall metal lattice-work. At either side of the lattice-work was a swinging, gate-like affair. The purpose of this became obvious after a moment as, swinging the left-hand gate shut and automatically locking it, the Amazon II had thus imprisoned Mexone in a metal cage from which he could not possibly escape.

This done she turned to Viona, removing her gun in readiness as she did so. A touch on a switch and the clamps holding Viona unlocked themselves. Surprisingly weak, she lurched forward unsteadily, to immediately find Amazon II at her side. Viona did not attempt anything. She had not sufficient strength.

Inevitably she found herself pushed into the second "gate" section of the strange apparatus and the tail grille slammed shut upon her.

"There are various ways of destroying you," Amazon II said briefly, reholstering her gun, "but this is probably the most efficient—electrocution. You, Viona, will doubtless understand what this apparatus is. Between the anode and cathode globes a tremendous voltage of artificial lightning will be generated. Though it may not actually destroy your physical forms, the current will certainly kill you, and I'll have your bodies disposed of later."

Since Viona did not say anything, Mexone kept quiet too. Amazon II waited a second or two, then obviously annoyed at the lack of reaction, she crossed to the switchboard and without hesitation pulled down the great plunger which released the stored-up current. A zigzag of lavender fire crackled its way through the "gates" between the globes and discharged itself on spiral towers reaching to the roof. Instantly Mexone and Viona collapsed helplessly to the bottom of their cages.

Amazon II smiled bitterly, restored the plunger, and then turned sharply as her observatory controller came hurrying in.

"Well, what is it?" she asked impatiently. "I'm very busy."

"This cannot wait, Amazon. A space machine has been sighted heading from the direction of Voldas and it is coming this way. It is identical in appearance to the earlier one we saw—the one used by the girl, Viona."

The controller's eyes strayed to the huddled figures, then back to Amazon II's grim face. Her violet eyes were puzzled.

"Are you sure of this?"

"Definitely so! You can come and look for yourself. I would warn you that this machine is approaching at a very high velocity— There is also another matter.

Voldas is returning to normal for the second time. The equilibrium process has again been upset."

"Then there's only one explanation," Amazon II said, her eyes narrowed in thought. "The only person I can think of is the Golden Amazon herself, and maybe Abna, too. Though how they got away from Jaxa I cannot imagine." Which was literally true. This was another of those instances where the spurious Amazon's capacity to reason failed her.

"You will come to the observatory then?" the controller asked quickly, but the second Amazon shook her head.

"No, your information is good enough for me and I have not a second to lose. I must deal with this advancing spaceship with the superior forces of the giant *Ultra*, and out in space is the best place to do it. Everything else must wait for the moment."

She turned quickly, almost pushing the controller out of the laboratory, after which she paused only long enough to operate the electronic lock on the blast-proof door. Then she raced at top speed through the long corridors, bound for the *Ultra* on the huge open space at the rear of the great building.

# CHAPTER NINETEEN
## VENGEANCE OF THE AMAZON

Meanwhile, aboard the tiny space ship, traveling with all the meager velocity of which it was capable—meager compared to the giant *Ultra* anyway—the Amazon and Abna were intently watching the exasperatingly slow approach of the inner world. Neither of them had any preconceived notions as to what they intended doing when they landed on the planet. The main question was whether they would ever get there at all, since, before long, they would be bound to be seen.

"So far we're safe enough anyhow," the Amazon commented, glancing at Abna by her side. "And once let me get my hands on that double of mine, and I'll tear her in pieces for what she's done to Viona!"

"We don't know the facts yet," Abna pointed out quietly. "Viona may still be alive—"

"You believe that?" The Amazon gave a brief, hopeless look. "I wish I could share your optimism. I'm reasonably certain that Viona is dead, and that young man Mexone—" She broke off and clenched her fists. "Why did it have to happen at such a time, Abna?

Viona evidently found the young man of her choice and then she dies, and he with her.... Yes, I meant every word I said as to what I'll do to my double when I get the chance!"

"From the look of things, the chance won't be long in coming," Abna said, watching space ahead intently. "Look!"

The Amazon concentrated her attention on the glittering speck at the left-hand limb of the inner world; then she turned quickly to the space ship's somewhat makeshift telescope. Weak though the lenses were, they were sufficient to transform the speck into the recognizable outlines of a space machine.

"The *Ultra*?" Ahna asked, and the Amazon looked up from the eyepiece and nodded.

"Yes—our own *Ultra*. Just as we feared, we've been spotted, and against the weapons there are in that ship we won't stand a chance. We've got to think of something quick."

Abna remained undisturbed, assessing the situation. Then: "Presumably it will be your double aboard the *Ultra* since she's the only one who knows how to control it. If we can find a way to make her captive out in space here and get aboard the *Ultra*, too, there are no limits to which we might not go. You might even take her place without anybody on the inner world being the wiser."

"Talk sense!" the Amazon said impatiently. "We can't possibly get aboard the *Ultra*. Every move we make will be watched, and we'd be blown to bits before we could even attempt it."

"If we did everything in the normal way, yes, but we've still a few tricks in the bag of which your double knows nothing. Metaphysical tricks, for instance."

"Meaning?" the Amazon asked, her eyes brightening.

"Meaning that with sufficient expenditure of mental energy I could instantly transport the pair of us to the inside of the *Ultra*. There'd be no guesswork about it since I know exactly how the *Ultra* is designed and the distance required for the 'manifested' leap would be easily calculated. Metaphysical science is one thing your double won't be expecting, I imagine."

"I'm all for it," the Amazon said, a trifle enviously. "I wish I had the gift myself, Abna."

"Maybe you will have when you develop more," he commented dryly, at which the Amazon gave him an indignant glance; then remembering the job on hand, she turned back to the outlook window and studied the approaching machine. Abna studied it, too, mentally computing the distance as it very gradually lessened.

"I think we're about ready now," he said finally. "If we leave it any longer we'll be within range of the *Ultra*'s weapons and then anything can happen. All right, get ready. Turn to face me."

The Amazon obeyed, her deep purple eyes looking steadily into Abna's. It was at times like this that she did not know the Abna of ordinary life: instead, she sensed the real power and majesty of his enormous intellectual attainments, heights which she knew she could not reach, despite her scientific brilliance. And, as she gazed, there crept over her a sense of profound drowsiness, accompanied by a slow fading of the ship's interior and the predominant vision of Abna's unwinking blue eyes.

Then darkness, a conviction of overwhelming cold, and what seemed to be a swift flight through the reaches of infinity. In a matter of seconds her full senses had returned and she realized she was in the main corridor of the *Ultra*, with the control room at the far end. Beside her, Abna was standing, slowly withdrawing his gun from his belt.

"Not bad, considering I'm out of practice," he murmured. "I missed the control room by a few yards, but at least we're safely within the ship. Now to surprise our lady friend."

The Amazon said nothing. She was silently digesting the marvel of such absolute control over the forces of matter—this practical demonstration of the higher power of mind—then she followed Abna down the passage until they reached the open door of the huge control room. Here they paused, impressed by the vaguely amusing sight of Amazon II peering through the great observation window toward the distant view of the now empty space ship in the distance. Under her fingers were the buttons of the *Ultra*'s atomic guns ready for immediate action.

"Leave this to me," the Amazon whispered. "Keep me covered."

Abna nodded, grinned faintly, and waited.

The Amazon crossed the control room with catlike stealth. A foot behind Amazon II she stopped and tapped the woman sharply on the shoulder.

Thoroughly startled, Amazon II swung round, and at the same instant the Amazon herself slammed out her right fist with all the frightful power of her arm. Nearly unconscious, Amazon II crashed to the floor and lay there, tumbled blonde hair cascading down her face.

"That's just a start," the Amazon explained, coming over to her. "Here's another sample—"

She seized the front of Amazon II's tunic, whirled her to her feet, then smashed up an uppercut that brought the sound of disintegrating bone. Her jaw fractured in two places, Amazon II dropped flat on the floor and lay there, completely knocked out.

"When she comes to," the Amazon said, flexing her fingers, "I'll keep my promise and take her apart by inches...."

Abna sighed and shook his head as he crossed the control room. He checked the course, set the *Ultra* so that it was heading back towards the inner world, then looked at the Amazon in reproof.

"Just your one trouble, Vi: every now and again you revert to type and lash out without reason!"

"Without reason!" The Amazon glared at him. "There was never a better reason!"

"I disagree. We don't know a thing yet concerning Viona, and if you knock your double about much more she'll be in no fit condition to tell us anything. I'll straighten her out and then you can start questioning her."

The Amazon became silent, her own inclinations entirely at variance with those of Abna. In a matter of minutes his metaphysical powers had not only restored her to consciousness but had healed her broken jaw as well.

"Better?" Abna inquired calmly, straightening.

She looked up at his towering height. "Yes. I'm better. How did you get aboard? You and my original?"

"No business of yours," the Amazon retorted, striding over. "Now, before I deal with you properly, where is my daughter and the young man Mexone?"

Amazon II was silent for a moment, then she gave a hard smile.

"Dead. And I'm glad of it. I electrocuted them. Now you can do as you like with me. I know when I'm beaten by superior force."

The Amazon clenched her fists and her face tautened in murderous fury. Definitely she would have hurled herself on her double there and then, only Abna's powerful hand caught her arm.

"Have you forgotten that we're crusaders, intent on spreading peace and happiness? Deliberate murder would entirely degrade the moral tone of our enterprise."

"Oh, stop talking from the heights of Olympus!" the Amazon snapped. "We have this mental parasite right here in our grasp—the mainspring behind every-thing—and you propose we should let her go free!"

"I didn't say that," Abna corrected patiently. "I said we should draw the line at murder. I'll explain in a moment."

He turned back to the cynically smiling Amazon II who had been listening to the conversation. Without any ceremony he bent down abruptly, hauled the surprised woman over his broad shoulder, and then carried her, kicking and shouting furiously, across the control room. Within a few minutes she had been dumped in one of the main storage holds and Abna locked the door upon her.

"Now," he said, coming back into the control room, "let's get things straight before we land on the inner world. Things are in the mess they are because your double exists on the thoughts you yourself radiated fifty years ago. Correct?"

"That's old history," the Amazon sighed, her arms folded. "We'll do no good until we destroy her and all she stands for. If you'd only let me have my own way, I'd kill her—with no more qualms than killing a tigress. That way we'd remove the mastermind from the inner world—and free this system from her domination—and also be avenged for the death of Viona and Mexone. But no...you have to be a godlike saint and forgive."

"Viona was my daughter as much as yours, Vi, and I'm no saint. We can still achieve our end without actual murder. If this woman's brain is surgically operated upon so she is unable to receive thoughts any,more the job is done. She is only what she is because of her mentally parasitic ability to pick up the thoughts radiated by you when you were back on Earth and amplified by Earth's own magnetic field. Destroy that capacity and she will still live—but as little better than an idiot. That is all these people of the inner world really are, remember—mindless dolts, living only by the dull instinct of the amoeba. That they seem brilliant, thinking people is because they have parasitic brains. By my method we do not kill. We merely deprive the leader of her mental power—which isn't really hers, anyway—and convert her into what she should be."

The Amazon considered for a long time, then at length a faintly sadistic gleam came into her eyes.

"I like it," he said softly. "I like it immensely.... It is infinitely crueler than actual killing."

"I suppose it is," Abna admitted, "but from the technical point of view it is not murder, and that is the main point."

"There is only one thing lacking in the plan," the Amazon continued. "She certainly will be finished as a ruling power. Probably, too, we can overcome the minions who so slavishly follow her and represent such a danger. But as the years go by there will be a man somewhere who will pick up your thoughts, from the time you came on Earth. That man will arise as Abna the Second, an even greater danger than this spurious imitation of me."

"Thanks for admitting I'm better than you," Abna grinned, with that odd reversion to boyishness which often pervaded him.

"I'm stating facts now—and it is an inevitable possibility. How do we meet it?"

"For the moment I don't know. Our major concern is to deal with this second Amazon, and we'll do it in the way I've said. When we reach the inner world you will pretend to be her. Listen carefully: this is what we'll do...."

# CHAPTER TWENTY
## VIONA REVIVES

Some fifteen minutes after Amazon II had hurriedly left the laboratory, securely locking the door behind her, Viona stirred slowly on the floor of the cage in which she was imprisoned. Thoughts and life were coming back to her—nor were they thoughts of pain or near-death. On the contrary, it was just as if she had been suddenly stunned into a deep sleep and was now awakening.

Cautiously she opened her eyes and looked about her, and her immediate reaction was one of joy at discovering the laboratory empty. She could not understand why it should be so, since she had fully anticipated that Amazon II would finish off the job she had started and dispose of the bodies. However, there was no point in looking a gift horse in the mouth, so Viona slowly struggled to her feet, grasping the bars of the cage to haul herself up.

This done, and her strength fast returning, she looked across at Mexone in the neighbor cage. To her relief he seemed to be unharmed as far as his body was concerned, even though parts of his clothing had been heavily scorched. At the moment he was essaying the effort to rise.

Viona looked down at herself, saw that her flying kit was burned into holes in several places, and then she looked about her at the twin globes. After thinking for a moment or two she called across to Mexone.

"On your feet, Mexone. You're still in one piece."

"So it seems," he admitted, straightening up. "Though I can't think why I should be. You, too—not even scratched. Yet our clothes are so burned away we're hardly decent. How do you account for it?"

"Acclimatization," Viona answered, shrugging. "Remember some time ago how you asked me how I could stand such high voltages without harm? I'm so used to absorbing electricity in various experiments I've built up a high resistance to it. That's a common law of physics in regard to organic bodies. An enormous resistance can be built up by gradual increase from small doses. All that happened when that current struck me was to knock me out—but it didn't kill, even if it did destroy most of my clothes."

"I can understand all that, Viona, but what about me? No reason why I should be resistant, is there?"

"There almost certainly is!" Viona was testing the bars of the cage as she spoke. "You received your resistance build-up in a different way—when paralysis overlook your planet. The amount of energy you must have absorbed—and lost—in having your molecular make-up brought to a standstill would make you even more resistant to current than myself, come to think of it. Amazon II couldn't have chosen a less efficient way of disposing of us."

"Queer she didn't think of that."

Viona laughed shortly. "There are a lot of queer things about that woman. Something urgent must have called her away. Our job is to get out of this mess before she comes back."

If Mexone considered this a forlorn hope he did not say so openly; but after a while his feelings underwent a change as he stood watching Viona. To his astonishment he saw that the strong bars of the "gate' which imprisoned her were slowly commencing to bend under the repeated attacks she made up them with her hands. Each time she returned to the task, the bars bent farther and farther away from each other until at last she could reach her arm through the space she had made. In this position, grasping the adjacent bar, and bracing the nearer one against her shoulder, she tugged and strained with all the strength of her muscles until there was a gap wide enough to just permit of her slim body sliding through. Little by little she eased herself through the gap and at last was free.

"You're the strongest girl I've ever seen," Mexone remarked in admiration.

"Like mother, like daughter." Viona smiled, and set to work on the bars of his own cage until she had forced a gap big enough for him to escape through it and join her.

"What happens now I'm not quite sure," she said. "Neither of us is armed, and just anything can lie beyond that door. Wonder if there are any spare guns anywhere?"

They immediately went on a search of the laboratory, but were unsuccessful in finding anything serviceable. At which Viona gave a shrug.

"All right—have to rely on our ingenuity—and my strength."

Mexone looked troubled for the moment. Though a normally powerful man, he felt his male status had been considerably besmirched, albeit not intentionally. He had reached the door with the electronic lock that Viona was carefully examining. After a long study of it she had to admit defeat.

"Nothing I can do here. All the human strength in the world wouldn't be able to smash open a door like this. Nothing short of a disintegrator gun, and we haven't got one."

"What about those anode-cathode globes which were turned upon us? They're on portable stands and connected by extra long lengths of cable."

Viona turned and looked at them, her eyes brightening. Then she snapped her fingers.

"Mexone, I believe you've got something!"

His eyes revealed his satisfaction at having proven himself useful at last; then at Viona's next words he looked disconsolate again.

"The two spheres as they are won't be any use, but we might be able to make use of the positive one. It should have a separate discharge point for its positive energy in case it builds up too much potential. If we connect that discharge-point to the door, it would probably vaporize it, or at least melt a good deal of it."

"All right; let's try it."

They hurried over to the tall pillars that supported the spheres and Viona examined them critically. After a few moments she was satisfied that both of them—as she had expected—were mobile. It would simply be a matter of disconnecting various cables and then unbolting the positive globe from the floor fixtures. Since the nearby tool racks over the main bench was provided with all manner of spanners, wrenches, and gadgets, this did not present any problem either. Mexone went to work on the unbolting while Viona severed those cables that she did not deem necessary. When they dragged the heavy stand into position, its discharge point—fashioned rather like a long, insulated rod—rammed against the door itself.

"Ready?" Mexone asked tensely, but Viona did not reply immediately. She appeared to be thinking something out. Finally she said:

"I have another idea, probably the best one yet. If we try and escape from here, we're sure to run into trouble because we have no weapons, but sooner or later the second Amazon is bound to return. When we see her start to open the door we can discharge the current. By all the laws of science we'll both electrocute and blast her. Even if she has enough resistance to stand up to it, she'll be knocked out long enough for us to get her guns: then we can escape and work everything out when we're on the move. Our job will be to get to the

*Ultra* somehow."

"Yes—sounds reasonable," Mexone admitted.

With Viona he moved over to the switchboard, there to keep up the vigil until the moment should arrive for the laboratory door to open.

# CHAPTER TWENTY-ONE
## REUNION

And it was a couple of hours after the young people had come to their decision that the great *Ultra* came sweeping down from the heights and landed smoothly at the "London" airport, only a few yards from the smaller *Ultra*.

"Ready?" Abna asked quietly, switching off the power plant.

"Quite ready." The Amazon gave a grim smile and took a newly replenished gun from her belt. "You are my prisoner—hence the gun—and I am Amazon II. The gun can be used for our defense if need be."

Abna pressed the airlock switch, waited for the huge door to open, then stepped outside. With the Amazon close behind him, her gun leveled, he strode across the open space of the airport, doing his utmost to assume the air of a beaten captive. In the distance, ground crews watched silently, not in the least suspicious of the occasion.

So, still without trouble, the central headquarters building was reached, and here again the Amazon moved with complete assurance, knowing from the actual time of her own past just how the building was designed. She gained her office, entered, then with a sigh of relief closed the door.

The Amazon switched on the intercom and tuned it to the main transmitting room. "The Amazon is speaking. Have Mr. Wilson and Miss Grayson come to my office immediately."

"Yes, Amazon," a voice responded promptly.

The Amazon gave Abna a hard smile and then sat back to wait. He remained by the desk, assuming again his "beaten captive" act when at length the door opened and Irene Grayson entered. Not long after her came Chris Wilson II, then when he also was seated the Amazon stirred herself in the chair.

"You two, along with me, represent the government of this city, do we not?" she asked, knowing full well from her earlier experience that this must be so.

"Yes—we do," Wilson II answered, without enthusiasm.

"You take your orders from me, and you obey them because there is no other alternative. Allowed free rein, you would probably handle things very differently. Am I right?"

Wilson II exchanged a puzzled look with the second Irene Grayson.

"I asked a question!" the Amazon snapped. "Answer it!"

"If you wish frankness," Irene Grayson said coldly, "we would revoke every one of your orders and give the people a chance to live in peace. I believe—and

I think Mr. Wilson does too—that your methods are altogether too savage for the well-being of the people."

"Which means you would like to see me removed?" the Amazon asked, with a grim smile.

"Unfortunately you have the power, Amazon, and we have not," Wilson II replied. "Why waste time on what can never come about?"

"I am led to believe," the Amazon continued, "that you have a very powerful underground movement aimed directly at me and my regime. Given the slightest opportunity you would put that movement into action and destroy everything I've built up."

There was silence. For the Amazon this had been a shot in the dark, but she was remembering that back in her earlier career such a shadow army had existed, waiting to pounce—so by all the laws of duplication it should exist now."

"What is the purpose of all this questioning?" Irene Grayson asked finally. "Certainly you have a great deal of secret opposition, which considering your general scientific brutality isn't to be wondered at."

"Thank you," the Amazon said calmly. "You have both satisfied me that you are not in favor of the present regime and that you would do anything to break it."

Wilson II gave a weary smile. "Which means death for the pair of us, I suppose, now you've found out?"

"On the contrary, I am hoping it will mean freedom. Forgive the interrogation, but I am not Amazon II. She is at present a captive in the *Ultra*. I am the original Amazon, and therefore very definitely on your side in the crusade against scientific domination."

For a moment Wilson II and Irene Grayson looked joyously relieved, then the shadow of doubt crossed their faces again.

"Naturally, the identical appearance between myself and my double makes it hard for you to be convinced," the Amazon said, getting to her feet. "You can take the word of Abna, though. Since his powers are immensely superior, even to my own, he would never confirm my identity if it were not true. Speak up, Abna."

He relaxed from his "captive" attitude and turned to the two.

"Absolutely true, my friends. This is my wife—the real Golden Amazon. Your spurious leader is locked up in the *Ultra*. This whole thing was contrived deliberately to test you, even to the point of my assuming the air of a prisoner. Even the questions were formed with the purpose of testing whose side you were on."

"But this is wonderful!" Irene Grayson exclaimed, jumping up with shining eyes. "It means the end of your double's rule, the end of our bowing and scraping to her wishes."

"That too is planned out," the Amazon assented "but for the time being the general populace must not know my real identity. I had to divulge it to you two so that you can put in action the opposing forces which must destroy my double's more or less loyal following."

"That can be done quickly enough,' Wilson II said, raising. "In a matter of twelve hours, maybe less, the followers of the second Amazon can be rounded up and her various scientific powerhouses put out of action. We know exactly where they are. As to the second Amazon herself, I assume you mean to kill her?"

"No." The Amazon shook her head "I was intending to do so, but my husband pointed out that killing is not in the code of the Crusaders—"

"But nothing else can be certain!" Irene Grayson protested. "As long as she is allowed to live, she will remain a menace."

"There is another way," the Amazon said quietly. "We shall destroy her power to absorb thoughts. That demands a surgical operation, and for that again your help is needed, I want you to get the best brain surgeons in the city together in the nearest operating theatre, and I will come and direct them as to what they must do. Are they behind my double or not? Whose side do they favor?"

"That is problematical," Wilson II said, thinking. "I think they can be classed as neutral. Like most medical men, they don't take sides."

The Amazon nodded. "I expected that. That being so, they must think I'm my double, and that the double on which they will operate is me. Get busy and summon them right away, Mr. Wilson, and then let me know which operating theater I must visit. My double will he brought from the *Ultra* bound and gagged—gagged so she cannot shout out the truth—and those who may chance to see her as she is conveyed to the operating theater must not have any hint of the truth until the job is done. Meanwhile, Miss Grayson, I leave it to you to set the opposition in action."

"Rely on it," Irene Grayson promised, and turned to follow Wilson II to the door, until the Amazon's voice called her back.

"There is one other thing," the Amazon said, her face hard. "My double told me that my daughter Viona—and a young man with her by the name of Mexone—were both electrocuted by her before she set off into space. Do you know anything about it?"

"Nothing at all. The second Amazon would hardly tell us in any ease."

"You've no record of what happened to them after the electrocution, I suppose? If their bodies could be found, metaphysical recovery from death might be possible."

Irene Grayson shook her head. "I haven't the faintest clue concerning them. The electrocution would be performed in the second Amazon's own laboratory, I suppose, and presumably she would dispose of the bodies there, granting any were left after the electrocution process.... Now, shall I depart to carry out your orders, or would you like me to direct you to the laboratories? Perhaps you'd like to have a look for some signs of your daughter?"

"I intend to look," the Amazon replied, "but I don't need to detain you. I know exactly where the main, laboratory is. Come, Abna."

They followed Irene Grayson out of the headquarters, and while she went off down the corridor to put opposition armies in motion, the Amazon led the way down the vistas in what she knew was the direction of the major laboratory. And her guess was right. Reaching it, she paused and studied the complicated lock. Then she made a wry face.

"Electronic lock, just as mine was back in time. To open it I shall have to remember the combination. Logical to assume that since my double has used my thoughts she would devise the same combination as I did for this lock. Let me think now...."

She stood pondering, Abna at her side, both of them unaware that on the other side of the door searing death was waiting. Viona and Mexone were still there by the switchboard, watching the door, and becoming unutterably bored.

"I believe," the Amazon said at length, "the combination is fourteen right, three left, and seven right again."

She took hold of the lock's control knob and adjusted it very carefully over the numbers she had quoted. At the end of the left-right movements there was a faint click.

"Good! My memory hasn't failed me. Now let's see what there is."

She pulled the door open wide towards her and gazed into the laboratory, straight into the amazed eyes of Viona and Mexone, both of them standing by the switchboard in their threadbare clothes. It struck the Amazon at that moment, even through her infinite relief at seeing Viona unharmed physically, that she had never seen such disappointment on anybody's face. Then the disappointment changed to joy as Abna loomed into view behind the Amazon.

"Mother.... Is it you?" Viona moved forward slowly, uncertainly.

"Yes," the Amazon smiled. "You need have no fear."

There were moments of embrace, even of tearful breakdown by Viona.

"Thank heaven, mother! Thank heaven—Everything else can wait for the moment. You'll never know how near I came to killing you, and father, too, perhaps."

"Killing us?" The Amazon looked puzzled, then she glanced at the nearby globe on the pillar. "With that, do you mean?"

"Yes—yes, with that!" Viona was laughing now with a touch of hysteria. Her words came tumbling on top of each other. "I'd arranged it so that when Amazon II came in, she'd push the door against the discharge point of the globe—only the door opens the other way! The other way! I didn't know that: I assumed it opened inwards! I was unconscious when Amazon II left here so I had no chance to notice, and I didn't remember which way it moved when we were first brought in here: I was too scared. The other way!" she finished, nearly doubling up in merriment.

"Thank heaven it does," Abna said, putting his arm round the girl's shoulders. "And take it easy, my dear. You're letting reaction get the better of you."

The Amazon watched her for a moment and then looked at Mexone.

"Well?" she asked him. "Maybe you can tell us what

happened, young man?"

He did so, with comparative calmness, and by the time he had finished Viona had recovered under the strong mental compulsion of her father.

"So her electrocution effort entirely misfired," the Amazon commented, smiling in relief. "Had she reasoned the thing out carefully, she'd have known that it would—but fortunately the power of intricate reasoning is not one of her accomplishments."

"Where is she now?" Viona asked urgently. "What's happened? Where have you and dad been all this time?"

"Come along to the private headquarters and I'll tell you. You two look as If you need food, rest, and then fresh clothes."

# CHAPTER TWENTY-TWO
## BRAIN OPERATION

An hour later, having had a meal, a rest, and now attired in fresh clothes brought from the *Ultra*, Viona and Mexone were in the big private office listening to the final details of the Amazon's story. With the piecing together of both adventures they could appreciate how the trend of events had combined to bring all of them safely together again.

"Then," Viona asked, "our present job is done when you have made Amazon II's brain incapable of receiving thought waves?"

"I would like to think so," the Amazon replied slowly, "but there still exists a very great danger which I've already mentioned to your father. Reducing my double to her normal state of near-idiocy does not remove the threat of scientific domination from this system, even though that threat cannot appear for some years yet."

"Oh?" Viona frowned. "What threat can there be?"

"I am the threat, my dear," Abna explained, somewhat ruefully. "In a few years these mental parasites will have caught up with the time when I arrived on Earth and gave your mother a run for her money. Somebody here will pick up those thoughts of mine, and if they have no sense of restraint—which is not very likely since these people have no normal emotions of their own—almost anything can happen."

"I see," Viona responded slowly, thinking. "And I suppose if it comes to that, almost anybody here could pick up the thoughts of whatever dominant people appear on Earth?"

"That's it," the Amazon conceded.

"Including my own thoughts?"

"Yes. Some young woman here will have a brain in sympathy with yours and eventually catch up. She could turn into a very real menace, as much a menace as my own double."

"The worst menace of all," Viona said, musing, "would be the one to pick up the thoughts of my late husband, Sefner Quorne."

Abna gave the slightest of starts and the Amazon shot him a quick look.

"We'd forgotten him," she said. "Anybody here emulating Quorne would be a terrifying prospect since he stopped at nothing and had the necessary scientific skill to back up his ruthless ambition.... Abna, the destruction of my double is only half the battle. We shall still have to think of a way to make this system safe before we leave it."

"We will," Abna responded, confident as ever. "Just a matter of thinking about it—"

He paused as there came a tap on the door and Wilson II came in. He looked across at the Amazon.

"I have made the necessary arrangements with the surgeons, Amazon, and they are waiting in Number One Operating Theater. Do you know where it is?"

"I know, yes. Thanks; I'll come at once."

The Amazon wasted no more time, but before going to the operating theater—Viona and Mexone going ahead to await her arrival—she and Abna returned to the *Ultra* and brought from the storage chamber the struggling, kicking Amazon II, her mouth heavily gagged and her wrists lashed behind her back with wire-cord strong enough to defeat her iron muscles.

Once taken from the *Ultra*, she was forced into a waiting atom-car, watched from a distance by a squad of ground-crew men who wondered vaguely what was transpiring—then the trip to the city's central hospital was completed in record time. The assembled brain surgeons, three of them, stood watching in silence as the angry woman, her violet eyes glaring in fury, was bundled into the theater, the Amazon and Abna on either side of her.

"Anesthetic!" the Amazon ordered, as by main strength she forced her double down flat on the nearest operating table.

The anesthetist went to work with calm efficiency, and at last the woman's struggles ceased. She lay motionless, her eyes closed. Only then, when assured she was thoroughly under, did the Amazon remove the gag and the wire-cord and cast a brief glance at Wilson II who had silently entered.

"I assume," the Amazon asked, looking at the head

surgeon, that Mr. Wilson has outlined my intentions?"

"He stated that you intended to have us perform a brain operation on this Earth-born double of yours, Amazon. We know no more than that." The head surgeon's eyes strayed to Abna. "I must confess to a certain bewilderment that this man, the husband of the woman lying on the table here, should stand passively by, and even help you in dragging this woman in here,"

This was a point that in the struggle to bring in Amazon II both Abna and the real Amazon had over-looked. Working in unison with each other, they had forgotten Abna's "captive" act.

"I'll be absolutely frank with you," the Amazon said, sensing the danger that might possibly develop if she did not take the plunge. "This is not the Earth-born Amazon: I am she. With my help you have it in your power now to render her incapable of further control."

"Thank you. It is better to know from the beginning how we stand."

"My hope is that you will cooperate," the Amazon went on quickly. "If you do not, I can force you to do so by scientific methods, even by hypnosis if necessary, but that isn't what I want. My husband, daughter, and I are Crusaders, not destroyers. Our aim is to liberate, not dominate. What have you to say? As men of medi-cine, you should be completely impartial."

"We are," the surgeon replied. "But in this case we are prepared to fight with you, not against you. We have suffered much under this madwoman's regime, and her deposition would be to the benefit of everybody. What do you plan to do?"

The Amazon relaxed, satisfied that her point had been won—then almost immediately she went into an outline of scientific surgery to which the three experts listened in grave silence.

"If you will direct, we will follow," the surgeon said finally, and he and his colleagues then went through the preliminary processes of disinfection and donning their facemasks and smocks.

From this point onwards, Viona, Mexone, Wilson II, and Abna all watched in silence the amazing intricacy of the surgery performed under the shadowless globes. The Amazon, masked and gowned like the surgeons, gave constant directions with the electric instruments, and in places, took a hand herself.

Probes, radiations, electronic reactors connected to the convolutions of Amazon II's naked brain, were all brought into use. For an hour she lay supine under the powerful anesthetic, then the trepanned section of the skull was returned to position and cellular substance, capable of immediate cohesion, was applied round the hardly visible lines of fracture. For the rest there was only a light bandage and the job was done.

"And you believe this will have the desired effect?" the head surgeon asked, mopping his face with a towel.

"It cannot fail to have!" The Amazon looked intently at the beautiful face, a complete replica of her own. "Her brain is now deprived of the section which enabled it to be parasitic to the thoughts of another. The woman who awakens will be a genuine inhabitant of this planet—as all of them would look if their parasitic mental power were destroyed."

"It will be interesting to observe," the surgeon said, with the cold detachment of his profession. "When do we administer the restorative?"

The Amazon glanced at the instruments. "There is no reason why it shouldn't be done now. Her heart can stand it."

The surgeon nodded, applied the restorative by injection, and then stood back to watch. Silently his two fellow-surgeons drifted to his side. To their left, the Amazon, Abna, Viona, Mexone, and Wilson II stood in a little group, intent and interested.

Amazon II stirred but slowly as the restorative took possession of her bloodstream; then gradually as dawning consciousness came to her, her general expression changed. The serene beauty of the feature under anesthetic assumed life, and with this there was a gradual metamorphosis from beauty to one of plainness, and presently even ugliness.

"This is horrible," the chief surgeon whispered, but nobody spoke.

Amazon II opened her eyes. They were still deep violet in color, but the fire of borrowed intelligence had gone. Instead they were dull and misted, reflecting a mind that had little comprehension of what was transpiring.

The woman put her tongue out quickly and then let it roll uncontrolled at the side of her mouth. A tiny trickle of saliva ran down her chin.... She stirred with the undisciplined movements of a baby and mumbled something unintelligible.

"An imbecile," the surgeon whispered. "A mindless dolt."

"Exactly," the Amazon confirmed, glancing at him. "And in her there is a grim warning for all of you on this world. At root every one of you is like she is now, but the strange quirk of nature that gives you the power to steal thoughts has produced what appear to be intelligent people. If for any reason that gift failed you, this parasite planet would be populated by beings...like this."

Nobody spoke. The death of intelligence—even if it had been borrowed—was somehow terrifying to observe.

# CHAPTER TWENTY-THREE
## ABNA'S PLAN

Night was settling over the great city when the news reached the Amazon's headquarters, through Irene Grayson, that the opposition forces had silently and completely taken possession of the various scientific outposts, which the now deposed Amazon II had maintained.

"Naturally," Irene Grayson said, "Mr. Wilson and I will not let it stay like that. We'll gather those whom we know stand for sanity and ordered progress and let the advent of your double die a natural death. Unless...."

"Unless?" the Amazon prompted, looking at the woman in the soft lighting.

"Unless you, your husband and daughter—and this young man from Voldas—would care to stay here and aid us in advancing our civilization?"

The Amazon shook her head slowly.

"No; there are reasons why that cannot be. You already have a first-class civilization left to you by the activities of my double. Our work here is finished. We have important things to do: far-reaching crusades to carry out. In less than an hour we shall be on our way."

"To where?" Irene Grayson was looking disappointed. "Or is it a secret?"

"We are first returning to Voldas to inform them as to what has been happening here. Also we have to make arrangements for the marriage of Viona to Mexone.... After that we shall set off into the void, never to return."

"I see." Irene Grayson held out her hand. "Then this is goodbye?"

The Amazon shook hands and smiled. "I'm afraid it is. We shall have no need of returning."

One by one the party shook hands with Irene Grayson; then she turned to the door. Pausing, she looked back over her shoulder.

"Our eternal thanks for what you have done for us."

The door closed behind her and the Amazon stood in silence for a moment, her yellow fingers drumming on the edge of the big desk. Finally she looked at Abna.

"We've come to it now, Abna," she said. "We have to work out some way of preventing these people being able to pick up our thoughts, otherwise this peace will only be temporary."

"Why not leave them be?" Viona asked impulsively. "We have done our job. Let the future take care of itself."

"No." The Amazon shook her head. "That would be leaving the job half done—leaving the rest of the inhabitants of this hexagonal system to their fate when the doubles of your father, you, and Sefner Quorne arise."

"But, mother, if we prevent these people from living on the thoughts of others we'll reduce them to horrible mental wrecks like Amazon II."

"If that is their natural, normal state—which it is—there is nothing horrible about it, even though it looks it to our intelligent senses. It is discovering a way to do it that is the problem."

"A hexagonal system," Abna repeated slowly, lost in thought. "Six planets all following the same orbit, and this inner world on the inside of the hexagon."

"What about it?" the Amazon asked briefly.

"I don't know yet, but the fact of a hexagon suggests something to my mind. I'll have to think about it...."

Which was exactly what Abna did, plunging into one of those spells of profound concentration that held until they were halfway to Voldas.

"I believe I have a solution!" he exclaimed. "Come here, all of you."

The Amazon, Viona and Mexone, who had been watching Voldas through the big observation window, came across to him. They surveyed the table upon which lay a litter of papers covered with symbols and equations.

"I think," Abna said, "that the unique formation of this system gives us the answer, but I'll come to that part of it later. For the moment just toy with this idea: thought-waves are as vulnerable to heterodyning as radio and other waves. Right?"

"Right," the Amazon confirmed. "For all practical purposes they can be considered to fall into the category of other radiations. So?"

"We can prevent them reaching the inner world by heterodyning them, or more plainly superimposing across them an obliterating energy track, ceaseless in emission."

The Amazon pondered, then: "Possibly we could heterodyne the incoming thought-waves for a time, but I don't see how we could keep it up. If we directed the heterodyning emission from Voldas, we could only do it while Voldas was in a certain position in relation to the inner world. As it moved away the effect would be lost until the next time round. And to judge from calculations, that 'next time round' might be many years."

"All right. Conceive a heterodyne emitter on each of these six planets. They have a 'follow-my-leader' orbit. One follows the other at an unvarying distance— perpetually. If a heterodyne beam were projected from each planet to the one immediately ahead of it, that would form an entire circle of heterodyning beams—a curtain, if you will. Since the inner world is inside the circle of planets, the thought waves normally reaching it would be perpetually insulated, or if not that, then distorted so much as to be useless for absorption by those parasite-brains. Remember, too, that the inner world revolves in the same orbital plane as the six outer worlds, so it would never get above or below the curtain. Always dead center."

"It's right," Viona said, staring thoughtfully into space. "Absolutely right! Why, father, it's a masterpiece!"

The Amazon did not admit as much, but she was looking vaguely pleased as she weighed the theory up carefully. Only Mexone seemed at a loss.

"I don't quite understand the method," he confessed. "I know what a heterodyne does, of course: upsets or obliterates an incoming electromagnetic wave. But this planet-to-planet system has me puzzled."

"Very well," Abna smiled, "I'll make it very simple. Imagine six people in a circle, all an equal distance from each other, all walking forward and maintaining that distance. A revolving circle. Got that?"

"Easily. Then what?"

"Inside this circle imagine another person—or rather two. One of them is motionless in the exact center, and represents the sun. We can forget all about him. Near him is the second person. Let us assume this second person will die if a beam of light is trained on him. All right, we train our beam of light on him from outside the circle of promenading people—the six we first spoke of. Clear so far?"

"Go on."

"For the sake of our analogy, the beam of light represents the incoming thought waves, unshielded. Now, from each of the six promenading people a screen is unrolled, the one in front taking hold of the length held by the man behind. Obviously a complete screen results, from one man to the other. The beam of light is cut off from the inner man. Or, more exactly, the thought waves are cut off. The screens represent heterodyning emissions from planet to planet. An endless chain, forever insulating the inner world from incoming thought-radiations. Understand?"

"Yes!" Mexone's eyes were bright. "Yes, I understand now. And as long as the emission remains, the thought waves will be insulated."

"That's it," Abna agreed shrugging "It just can't fail. In no time the inhabitants of the inner world will revert to what they really are, as the Amazon II did. I know it means the end of their civilization, their devolution into a world of mindless idiots, but that cannot be helped. We're not reducing them to that: they revert to it by nature's law when their spurious form of intellect is cut off."

"But why keep it up perpetually?" the Amazon asked, thinking. "Wouldn't perhaps a week of that be enough to reduce them?"

"No. Once the power was released, their brains would again pick up thought waves—a week behind where they were! The emission must be perpetual, until a day comes when those mindless creatures die, or a change in evolution makes their brains incapable of stealing thought-waves."

"Mmmm, I see what you mean," the Amazon acknowledged. "Yes, Abna, the idea itself is sound enough, but it involves six worlds, and one of them is Carboniferous, as we have good reason to know. How do you propose to keep an emitter going on that world, for instance?"

"Remote control from Voldas. Remote control for each world, in fact. We must talk with the governments of the populated worlds, four of them excluding Voldas, and explain to them that their very future depends on them permitting us to fix an emitter. It won't interfere too much with their normal radio transmissions where they have any. Judging from the types of civilization the four other worlds seem to possess, I don't think we'll encounter much opposition."

"One more point," Mexone put in. "You speak of these heterodyning emitters being perpetual in action. How do you hope to achieve that? Won't they have to be recharged, or something, from time to time?"

The Amazon smiled. "In that, Mexone, you are speaking from the standpoint of your own—as yet—undeveloped science. We shall use solar power for the emitters, which will constantly draw on your sun for their energy."

"Even through thick cloudbanks?"

"Certainly. Clouds are barriers to light and, in less potent form, to heat—but not to radiation. That penetrates through everything except perhaps lead. Back on Earth everything is powered by solar generators. We'll demonstrate it to you later."

With that Mexone had to be satisfied—and in any ease there was no further time for talking since the surface of Voldas was rapidly approaching. Abna brought the *Ultra* down not far from Cesnon's residence, and before long the party had arrived within it.

A transmitted call to his emporium in the city was enough to bring him hurrying home urgently, and his relief at finding Mexone well and unharmed was more than obvious. When at last the joy of reunion was over the Amazon said:

"Up to now, Cesnon, you have been acting as the go-between for us and your government, and since you are a man of some prominence in the city, your requests are heeded. I want you to call a special meeting of your government so I may put certain proposals to them— proposals vital to your future safety."

"Of course," Cesnon agreed readily. "I'll do it immediately. But may I ask one thing: will the paralysis return for the third time?"

"That I can understand. You can tell your media, and anybody else you wish, that for a long time to come your world is safe, but that safety cannot be guaranteed as permanent until your government hears what I have to say."

Cesnon nodded. "I understand. I'll make the necessary arrangements right now."

"And in the meantime," the Amazon added, "my husband and I must trespass upon your good nature and become your guests...."

# CHAPTER TWENTY-FOUR
## THE METAMORPHOSIS OF MEXONE

Cesnon had no difficulty in having the benevolent government agree to an emergency meeting, which was fixed for the following morning—so for the first time in many months there came to the Amazon, Abna, and Viona an evening and a night when no demands were made upon them. More for the joy of it than anything else, they obtained normal civilized clothing from the *Ultra*, the Amazon and Viona in particular dressing themselves with exquisite taste, and then retired with the immaculate Abna to the lounge of the residence. It was one of those curious "earthly" moments when the strange odyssey of riding the stars was forgotten.

"I have always known Viona to be a beautiful girl," Mexone said, studying her in the soft lights, "but it has never been so apparent as now."

Viona gave a smile, almost a shy one, for her. The backless emerald-green gown she was wearing contrasted in absolute perfection with the copper-gold of her hair. Yet even so she was still outshone by the golden glory of the Amazon herself, still seeming no more than twenty-five, her tawny skin catching the delicate lighting, the flame silk of her gown giving an added sheen to her magnificent golden hair.

"As to that," the Amazon said, "it was suddenly sprung upon Abna and I that you two had decided to become engaged. Logically, you will shortly marry?"

"Obviously!" Viona replied, looking surprised. "What else did you expect, mother?"

"Nothing else, knowing that the young rarely think beyond the present moment—but have you considered all that it means? Just what are your intentions after marriage?"

"To work beside Mexone and build up the science of this planet into streamlined perfection. We laid the groundwork of that just before we set off into space to find you and father."

"I learned more marvels in a few weeks than I could have guessed at in a lifetime," Mexone put in. "Supersonic aircraft, the basis of atomic power, and space travel! Viona gave our engineers all those secrets before we left to find you."

"In that case," Abna said, "there doesn't seem to me to be much reason for you to stay behind and improve things, Viona. If the engineers have the basis, they'll finish things off for themselves."

A dim hint of indignation came into Viona's blue eyes as she considered first her father, then her mother.

"Just what are you two driving at?" she demanded finally. "It sounds very much to me as though you don't like the idea of my marrying and settling down."

The Amazon laughed. "My dear child, nothing

pleases us more than that you have found this excellent young man, but knowing your temperament I know for a certainty that you will never settle down. For a while maybe, then the urge will come to wander. To fly out into the void, to explore the myriads of mysteries of the universe, which are still unsolved. At heart you are a Crusader, like your father and myself, and nothing will ever change it."

Viona and Mexone exchanged looks—looks of such disappointment and bewilderment that even Cesnon joined in the laughter. His wife and young daughter looked on, smiling, at a loss because they could not understand the English language.

"It isn't funny!" Viona objected finally, pouting.

"It is when the answer is so simple." The Amazon smiled. "It doesn't mean you must part from Mexone. It means he must become a Crusader, too!"

Viona's mouth opened, but she did not speak. Mexone himself gave a start, and doubt leaped into his dark eyes.

"I, a Crusader? There is nothing I'd love better, but I'm afraid I'm not cut out for it. You three are giants in strength and intellectual knowledge. I'm just an ordinary young man of average development. I haven't yet forgotten how Amazon II manhandled me, and there was nothing I could do about it."

"But, dearest, those things don't matter!" Viona insisted. "We'd look after you!"

Mexone smiled faintly. "That's the part I don't like. As a man I ought to be able to look after myself—and you, too, Viona. I'd only be a drag on the three of you, and feeling it very keenly, too."

Abna smiled and looked at the young man with his steady blue eyes.

"Let's settle this once and for all, Mexone. First, it's plain now that you and Viona would both be willing to come with us into whatever new adventures await us. You in particular, Mexone, would be willing to leave this world of yours, and your parents, never to return?"

"With reluctance," Mexone sighed, glancing at his mother, father, and sister each in turn. "But I have my life to make. Yes, I'd forsake everything here because my scientific curiosity and love for Viona supersede any ties I have here."

"I don't see why we can't come back here once in a while," Viona remarked.

"We could, if we had not all the Universe in which to roam," Abna told her. "It is more sensible to face the fact that once we leave here, we'll never come back—just as we forsook Earth when we became the Crusaders. Progress lies in going ever forward, not returning to old standpoints.... But to get back to you, Mexone, having learned that you are willing, the solution lies in making you a Crusader as physically strong as we are. We can also give you immense scientific knowledge by mental transposition, much the same way as language was given to you. When that has been done, you will be a Crusader worthy of the name."

Mexone's expression was one of puzzled interest. "But is it possible to change me? A grown man?"

"Entirely possible," Abna replied. "It all lies in the build-up of the molecular structure and certain glandular changes, as far as the physical is concerned. You'll see later on. After the government meeting tomorrow, there may be a chance to go to work on you."

After which the topic veered to the time of Mexone and Viona's marriage; until after a certain amount of argument it was decided that it should be immediately after the heterodyne transmitters had been successfully installed on the neighboring planets.... So the conversation continued until far into the night; then the following morning the Amazon and Abna set off with Mexone, as interpreter, and Viona for their appointment in the governmental conference room. Nor did it demand much hard work on the Amazon's part to make this all-powerful body see the necessity for the heterodyne transmitters.

"You will have our full co-operation, madam," the president said—through Mexone—when everything had been explained. "I will issue an order to our engineers that whatever you may desire them to do must be done, as fast as possible. Am I to assume that the first transmitter will be installed on this planet?"

"That is so," the Amazon assented. "Not only the transmitter, but the major power house which will control all the other transmitters on the neighbor worlds. Once the solar power is at work, the transmitters will virtually work themselves, but if any fault should develop, your major powerhouse will know of it by the instruments installed for remote control.

Since you now have the answer to space travel, your engineers will be able to go and rectify whatever faults appear, though none should."

"So be it," the president acknowledged. "And our gratitude goes out to you all for what you have done to bring peace and progress to our system."

The Amazon smiled. "To be of service is the main object of our crusade. We will see to it that your engineers are thoroughly briefed as to what they must do."

The president nodded benevolently, which about brought the conference to a close. Thereafter, for the rest of the day, Abna—as the original creator of the heterodyne system—spent his time drawing detailed sketches and specifications of the apparatus required. These in turn were handed to the best engineers on the planet, while the Amazon for her part drew the plans of the powerhouse together with all its necessary fittings. To her fell the job of explaining to the architects what would be needed, and the choosing of the isolated site a little distance from the city. Definitely a mammoth program for one day, and yet by nightfall it was successfully finished, and Abna and the Amazon returned to the cordial atmosphere of the Cesnon household.

It was after a late evening meal that Mexone brought up the subject that was plainly uppermost in his mind.

"You mentioned, Abna, you would see what could be done about me. I know it's pretty late, but— Well, how about it?"

"Of course," Abna smiled. "Come along to the

*Ultra* where there is the necessary apparatus. We can leave the womenfolk behind, otherwise you might feel embarrassed."

Mexone grinned modestly and followed his giant father-in-law-to-be from the lounge. Twenty minutes later the private car had brought them to the open space where the *Ultra* lay, and very soon Mexone was glad of the fact that he and Abna were alone, chiefly because for the purposes of the operation it was necessary for the young man to completely strip. Thereafter he gave himself up with every confidence to Abna's skilled ministrations and lay motionless on a long table as various beams and radiations played upon him. He felt no actual pain, though there was definitely a constant sense of movement within him as glands changed their courses and muscles were relaxed or tightened. At the end of an hour he was commencing to feel the strain, at which point Abna ceased his activities.

"Well, that's it," he said, coming across. "In a couple of hours you will appreciate just how much difference has been made to your physique. Now get dressed, then we'll get busy on the mental part."

Mexone nodded quickly, already feeling a springiness about his limbs which he had never known before. Then when he had dragged his clothes on again, he seated himself under Abna's directions and thereafter went through a process very similar to the one when he had been taught the English language. But on this occasion the difference lay in the fact that scientific knowledge was conveyed to him by hypnotic means.

With every passing moment he became aware of scientific powers that he had never known existed, and what was even more remarkable, the knowledge showed no signs of fading.

"It never will fade," Abna said, when he ceased concentrating and Mexone mentioned the matter to him. "The thoughts you have received are indelible, and the knowledge is for you to use as and when necessity demands it. I have, of course, retained one or two secrets—or more correctly, I have not imparted them because they are individual to me and cannot be transferred to another. The mastery of metaphysics, for one thing."

Mexone rose slowly from the seat. "You have been kind enough as it is, Abna, without me wishing to take more. I assume that I now have the intelligence and the strength worthy of a Cosmic Crusader?"

"No doubt of it," Abna smiled, picking up a solid metal bar from the testing bench. "Here—see what you can do with this."

Mexone took it, holding it with a hand at each end. He knew full well that in the normal way he would never even have been able to bend it in the slightest degree, yet now without the slightest effort he twisted it into a circle, then for good measure finished it off with a bow.

"Good," Abna chuckled. "Now you'll be able to show that knowledgeable daughter of mine who's boss when you get married."

Mexone tossed the twisted bar down and reflected, a

touch of whimsy in his expression.

"By scientific means, Abna, you have turned me into a superman," he said slowly. "If you can do it with me, you can do it with others—women included, I suppose."

"Naturally." But there was inquiry in Abna's eyes.

"Well, then, why don't you? Why be content with just four in the party? The more Crusaders there are, the further you can spread your gospel of peace and achievement."

"It is not as easy as that, Mexone," Abna replied quietly. "Before either my wife or I would attempt the conversion of any man or woman into superbeings, we would have to be absolutely sure of their integrity, their inner motives—every little detail about them. With you, those details are perfectly clear. No, great power is only for the few, and those few must be capable of handling it wisely. Some day, perhaps, on some far world as yet undreamed of, we may find a race who exist purely on righteous motives. They are the kind to become superbeings and leaders of the lesser creatures."

Abna was silent for a moment or two, his thoughts in infinity; then with an apologetic smile he turned.

"Leave the dream to the future, Mexone, and let us take care of the present. We'd better return to the others and let them behold the transformation which has been produced in you."

And upon the return to the Cesnon residence, it was to Viona that Mexone presented the greatest wonder. To her young heart, completely captivated by this darkly handsome young man, the metamorphosis into a scientific superman on an equal with herself was something at which to marvel. To the Amazon—and, of course to Abna—it was commonplace, but that did not prevent them joining in the brief celebration with Cesnon and his family. A fourth Crusader had come into being, and before him lay the reaches of eternity.

"And our marriage shall consummate the miracle," Mexone said, smiling, after the drinks. "Sooner we get our neighbor worlds fixed up with heterodyne-emitters, the better I'll like it. How long do you think it will take, Amazon?"

"Not very long. I expect the engineers to have everything ready for the first planet within a week, so on that basis, let us assume six weeks or two months for everything—based on Earth time, that is. Since we have a free week, we'd better start to visit the neighbor worlds tomorrow and open up relations with them."

So, after breakfasting the following morning, the four set off on the brief journey to the next nearest world. Here they discovered an amenable civilization having a language that was easily understood. Since space travel was not among their accomplishments, the visitation of the four from the void seemed little less than miraculous. But once the wonder had gone and it was made clear to them that their future depended upon them conceding a fraction of their planet upon which an emitter could be erected, they willingly cooperated, particularly when they knew that the matter of maintenance was not their problem, but that of the "guardian world," as they insisted on naming Mexone's planet.

On to the next world, and here again the quartet repeated the same process. The civilization of this planet was of a fairly high order, with space travel just around the corner, and for some time there was obviously suspicion among the governing body as to whether the emitter might not be a disguised threat against them. That they were eventually convinced was solely owing to the eloquence and scientific illustration of the Amazon herself.

The remaining two worlds presented no difficulty at all. One had a low-grade civilization, whom it was simple to convince for the main reason that they could not even comprehend the nature of the danger and were overawed by these scientific geniuses who had dropped from nowhere. The remaining world has nothing but a Cro-Magnon type of life with whom communication was impossible. So a suitable site for the emitter was selected. Then followed the brief trip to the hell planet of Jaxa, also for the purpose of finding a good site. Once the emitters were erected on these wilder worlds, no form of life would be able to damage them, so invulnerable would be their construction.

Altogether, the visiting of the various planets and the arrangements entailed, occupied ten earthly days—which turned out to be nice timing, since upon return to Mexone's world it was found that the first emitter had been constructed and was ready for testing.

The results, tried out in the electrical laboratory,

were all that Abna had foreseen. The heterodyne emission was pitched at just the right frequency to offset the extremely short wavelengths generated by thought waves, while the solar generator, devised for absorbing and then transforming the perpetual energy of the system's sun, worked to perfection.

"Engineering plus," Mexone said in admiration, when the test was over. "And, to me, the delightful thing now is that I can understand the technicalities involved. Only one thing escapes me. In projecting the heterodyne wave from one planet to the other, what happens to it at the receiving end? I realize it forms a barrier between the worlds, but does it dissipate when it strikes the neighbor world at which it is aimed?"

"Normally it would," Abna answered, "but in this case, since there is a transmitter on each planet, that transmitter will be supplied with a receiver as well. That receiver will absorb the incoming heterodyne emission and neutralize it. Everything will have to be worked out with mathematical exactitude."

In this latter matter the *Ultra*'s computers were brought into action, and by their aid each desired position on each world was pinpointed; then began the task of visiting each world in turn, in company with construction engineers, to start the erection job.

The Amazon had considerably undercalculated the time that would be needed for this task. The emitters themselves were finished up to date and duly tested, but the delay came in the actual erection on the various worlds. There were geological difficulties, wild animals to cope with, dangerous terrain, but one by one the obstacles were overcome with the relentless determination which had once typified Earth's early pioneers Altogether it was eight months before the party returned to Mexone's world to make the final test for position, and to their relief the radar "echo" showed that every emitter was in its exactly right place in the follow-the-leader procession of the planets.

"Which means," Abna said, surveying the immense powerhouse that was to be the main unit of the whole emitter chain, "that there remains now only to switch on the power. When that happens, the heterodyne wave will flash from here to the next nearest world. The emitter on that world will start up and emanate its heterodyne, and so in a matter of minutes the whole neutralizing shield will be established, and remain for untold ages."

"At the very least," Mexone said, "it will remain until my people have reached the very peak of civilization and will then be able to offset for themselves whatever danger might threaten them."

Abna said: "Tomorrow, with all due ceremony, we will switch on the power. By evening tomorrow the inhabitants of the inner world, every single one of them, will be reduced to their natural state and the threat of that parasite planet wilt be destroyed for all time."

Nobody commented. Whatever ruthlessness might be apparent in the plan, it was offset by the realization that if it were not put into operation, tens of thousands of innocents in the future might suffer extermination at the hands of a scientific dictator. The facts remained: the people of the inner world were not being destroyed in the full meaning of the term. They were being returned to the state normal to them, and one from which they should normally only arise by progressive stages of evolution.

# CHAPTER TWENTY-FIVE
## REVERTED WORLD

It was early the following morning when the quartet entered the power house, accompanied by all the dignitaries of the planet's various governments. The short speech Abna made was in the people's own language, then he grasped the master switch and drove it home.

Immediately the immense power plant started up to a low whine, gathering force with the seconds, until by easy stages the maximum was reached in a deep purring. Abna turned from the switchboard, his face gravely triumphant.

"As far as we are concerned," he announced, "the job is done. The instruments show that the heterodyning power is being emitted exactly as planned, but the precise results can be ascertained in only one way—namely, by going to the inner world and seeing for ourselves. Since the effect of this heterodyning screen will be almost immediate, we shall certainly see its results by the time we get to the inner world if we leave within an hour."

Certainly nobody raised any opposition to this suggestion. Indeed, it was the only sure way of finding out if the inner world threat was actually finished for good. So within the hour the *Ultra* was on its way, carrying with it, in addition to the quartet, several government officials and the ever-interested Cesnon. To these latter the space journey was in itself a wonder not to be missed, so for them at least the time did not hang heavy.

To the quartet it was merely a routine trip. They wanted it over and done with so they could get their glimpse of a population denuded of intelligence. The *Ultra*'s instruments showed clearly enough that not a single short-wave radiation was passing through into this inner void inside the chain of six worlds, which in itself was evidence enough of the efficiency of the neutralizing curtain.

Then at length the inner world loomed visibly closer, the clouds scattered in its sunlit atmosphere and the pattern of cities beneath. Swiftly Abna brought the machine down and then opened the airlock. Without speaking, he followed the Amazon and Viona to the open portal, the government authorities coming up in the rear.

"From the sound of things, or rather the lack of it," the Amazon commented, "we've achieved our object."

What she meant had been apparent from the moment they had stepped out of the *Ultra*. There was a deadly calmness over the area in which they stood, and yet it was not the terrifying quiet produced by thermo-dynamic equilibrium. Here, the leaves of the trees moved in the soft wind. In the distance there whirled a subsiding eddy of dust—but from the city nearby, patterned so exactly after the London of the twenty-first century—there were no sounds whatever.

"Let's look further," Abna said briefly, and at that they all began moving, coming eventually to the main road adjacent to the open area in which the *Ultra* lay. And it was here that they beheld the first evidences of the change the heterodyne radiation had brought about.

Traffic had come to a standstill and within the vehicles there were dead men or women, or else drooling, fatuously smiling idiots to whom intelligence was a gift unknown. Those who had been injured in vehicle smashes seemed unaware of what had happened, and were apparently so low in the order of intellect they could not even feel pain or register it.

So the grim story continued to unfold itself in ever-greater significance. The city's streets and buildings were packed full of men, women, and children at the lowest level of comprehension, creatures who gazed with lackluster eyes at the visitors, and then turned away, disinterested and uncomprehending.

"Let's get out," Viona said at last, her face strained. "I have seen as much as I can take. The job's done: let it go at that."

Her parents and the government officials nodded silent assent and the exploration ceased therewith. Once back inside the *Ultra*, the party looked at one another.

"Even if we have only reduced them back to where they belong," Viona said slowly, "I still feel horribly guilty about it."

"You needn't," Abna told her. "A worm is not revolting because of its low-grade intellect: it is its natural state. So it is with these people. It is because we saw them evolving on stolen intelligence in the first instance that makes the opposite picture seem so unbearable now. However, I feel certain that within a few generations, these people will begin a slow, upward climb of their own. They are still basically human, and should therefore evolve naturally. What do you think, Vi?"

"Very likely—but that doesn't signify," the Amazon said, with her usual practicality. "Our work here is ended—"

"Not quite," Mexone said, smiling slightly. "The final consummation of your visit is our marriage...," and he hugged Viona closely to him.

The government officials looked on and smiled with Mexone, entirely ignorant of what he was saying.

"After which," Cesnon sighed, "it will be necessary to say farewell to you, my son, for all time. Your mother, sister, and I will miss you deeply."

"At least I shall have departed for a good purpose," Mexone said. "To spread the gospel of science and peace. What finer purpose than that?"

"True, true." But there was sadness in Cesnon's eyes as he looked out on the deeps of space. Then he turned to the Amazon and Abna. "And to where will you journey next, friends, when you take Mexone and Viona with you?"

"Wherever the spirit moves us," the Amazon smiled,

her violet eyes on the stars. "Out there are countless other systems, Cesnon, surrounded by worlds which probably contain living creatures. Every world and every system has something different to offer, but we shall only concern ourselves with those who live uneasily. To that end the Cosmic Crusaders were born!"

# ABOUT THE AUTHOR

British writer **JOHN RUSSELL FEARN** was born near Manchester, England, in 1908. As a child he devoured the science fiction of Wells and Verne, and was a voracious reader of the Boys' Story Papers. He was also fascinated by the cinema, and first broke into print in 1931 with a series of articles in *Film Weekly*.

He then quickly sold his first novel, *The Intelligence Gigantic*, to the American magazine, *Amazing Stories*. Over the next fifteen years, writing under several pseudonyms, Fearn became one of the most prolific contributors to all of the leading US science fiction pulps, including such legendary publications as *Astounding Stories*, *Startling Stories*, *Thrilling Wonder Stories*, and *Weird Tales*.

During the late 1940s he diversified into writing novels for the UK market, and also created his famous superwoman character, The Golden Amazon, for the prestigious Canadian magazine, the Toronto *Star Weekly*. In the early 1950s in the UK, his fifty-two novels as "Vargo Statten" were bestsellers, most notably his novelization of the film, *Creature from the Black Lagoon*.

Apart from science fiction, he had equal success with westerns, romances, and detective fiction, writing an amazing total of 180 novels—most of them in a period of just ten years—before his early death in 1960. His work has been translated into nine languages, and continues to be reprinted and read worldwide.

www.ingramcontent.com/pod-product-compliance
Lightning Source LLC
Chambersburg PA
CBHW050732250626
47155CB00005B/1759